A Candlelight Ecstasy Romance®

"MY MONEY IS EARNED.
I WORK FOR IT."

His words stung. To her family, Dana was practically a hobo. To Gary LeBlanc, she was one of the idle rich. "Excuse me," she said acidly. "I never learned to be anything other than a social butterfly. I'm a product of my environment."

"I could think of some use to put you to."

His hand was on her chin, tilting her head back so that her eyes met his. She had the dizzying sensation of drowning in their deep, velvety depths. She was immobile as his face swam before her, as his mouth, full and sharply defined, closed in on hers.

"Gary . . ."

"I want to be your lover," he said huskily.

It had been a long time since she'd felt the flames of desire raging, and never so furiously. . . .

A CANDLELIGHT ECSTASY ROMANCE ®

HEAVEN'S EMBRACE

Sheila Paulos

A CANDLELIGHT ECSTASY ROMANCE ®

Published by
Dell Publishing Co., Inc.
1 Dag Hammarskjold Plaza
New York, New York 10017

Dell ® TM 681510, Dell Publishing Co., Inc.

Candlelight Ecstasy Romance®, 1,203,540, is a registered
trademark of Dell Publishing Co., Inc.,
New York, New York.

ISBN: 0-440-13504-4

Printed in the United States of America
First printing—April 1984

To Our Readers:

We have been delighted with your enthusiastic response to Candlelight Ecstasy Romances®, and we thank you for the interest you have shown in this exciting series.

In the upcoming months we will continue to present the distinctive sensuous love stories you have come to expect only from Ecstasy. We look forward to bringing you many more books from your favorite authors and also the very finest work from new authors of contemporary romantic fiction.

As always, we are striving to present the unique, absorbing love stories that you enjoy most—books that are more than ordinary romance.

Your suggestions and comments are always welcome. Please write to us at the address below.

Sincerely,

The Editors
Candlelight Romances
1 Dag Hammarskjold Plaza
New York, New York 10017

CHAPTER ONE

Dana Manchester tried to yawn. Her face, under a mud pack hardened to the consistency of a plaster cast, would not move. She swallowed the yawn.

The cosmetologist, trained in Hungary, hummed a rhapsody as she dabbed cotton balls in mysterious solutions and expertly proceeded to remove the mask.

"You take a little bit more steam, Miss Manchester. Then I come back and we work again." The cosmetologist draped Dana's head with towels and helped her to lean over the kettle of vaporizing camomile leaves. Before the woman left the soundproofed mirrored cubicle she lowered the lights.

With her eyes closed Dana took deep gulps of the therapeutic herbal steam. She imagined her pores opening. She felt her nasal passages clearing. She thought of her mother telling her how lucky she was to be able to indulge in such luxury as a facial at Georgette Klinger, New York's celebrity-studded salon. Then her neck, strained from leaning sideward over the dental-style chair, began to hurt. When she opened her eyes she felt that she was sitting in the middle of a cloud, for her contact lenses were misted over. She wished she were sitting in a cloud, or at least reaching for one on Mount McKinley, instead of reclining in padded splendor. Almond scrubs, and mud packs by Olga or Marie, makeup by Jean-Louis or Jean-Pierre were really not for Dana Manchester. She had always been perfectly content with Dove soap and Maybelline. It was her mother who had pressed this series of three facials on her, insisting that it would break her maternal heart if her daughter refused the gift.

Her mother, Dana thought amusedly, was still trying to make a lady out of her. She had not yet accepted the fact that her daughter, at twenty-eight, was not going to change. Dana had always been considered a tomboy, though she had never thought of herself in those terms. She liked the out of doors, she liked sports, she liked being herself. She didn't like spending hours buying clothes, putting on makeup, or sitting at the hairdresser. She didn't like people who tried to impress one another by using long tablecloths at dinner parties and who let each other know, in carefully coded ways, how rich and happy they were. Dana Manchester, in the Scarsdale milieu in which she had been raised, was an oddball.

Throwing the towels off her head, then popping out her contact lenses, Dana stood up gingerly. This world of collagen and gold-leaf elevators was seductive in the way of silken cocoons. But Dana longed to fly. Actually she longed to climb. It was only because of the rejection she had gotten in the mail a couple of weeks ago that she had been dispirited enough to let her mother convince her to go for the unwanted facials. Sensing her advantage, her

8

mother cajoled her into a haircut at Cinandre, that ultra-swank establishment where an appointment meant the sacrifice of an entire afternoon. At Cinandre people didn't say hello to each other. *A la* the French they kissed on both cheeks. It was true, Dana had admitted, the haircut, precise and sharp, yet leaving her tresses long, was the best she had ever had. But she had been perfectly content with her chestnut hair plaited on top of her head. Perfectly content, she thought wryly as she slipped out of the dressing gown supplied by Klinger and into her own corduroy jeans. Perfectly content was something she had never been in Manhattan or in Scarsdale and only intermittently at her present home in Boston. It was a feeling she experienced mostly when scaling a hill or climbing a mountain. She was perfectly content when she felt her body working in harmony with her mind. She was happy when she didn't have to explain herself, when she could just be. In the resolutely affluent world where she had been born she was an enigma, the only one who preferred the clean smell of pine cones to the musky scent of Opium perfume.

To be a member of the climbing team which was going to tackle the "Great One," the Karstens Ridge of Mount McKinley which soars four miles in one unbroken sweep of rock and ice, was her dearest wish. There was nothing on earth she wanted more. That she should have had a good shot at making the team was clear to her. When she had gotten the form rejection letter it had been obvious that she had not even been considered, for she had the credentials and the experience. What she didn't have was the right sex. As a group, mountain climbers were not male chauvinists. Many of them, pro-ERA types, were happy to climb with women whose talent they respected. But there were some teams that rigorously excluded women from participating, jealously guarding their expedition as an impenetrable bastion of sexism. It had been the worst luck that this team headed by Gary LeBlanc was as misogynistic as they got. And it was so unfair.

She clenched her fists. For the past five years Dana had been climbing, learning, and perfecting techniques. She was superb. Perhaps she wasn't as strong as a man, but she more than made up for it with finesse. She had accomplished difficult ascents, including most of the challenging climbs in the eastern United States as well as those in the Rockies and Tetons. There were two world-class mountains in the continental United States. One was Mount Rainier in Washington, which she climbed regularly. The other was Mount McKinley in Alaska. These were mountains that would sorely test the skill of even Himalayan climbers or of those who tackled the forbidding peaks of the Chilean Andes. Until modern times, with its complicated equipment and techniques, McKinley had been successfully scaled by no more than two teams. Even today, more often than not, highly skilled teams failed to take the summit. The Karstens Ridge of McKinley called for infinite skill, endurance, and courage.

The door of the cubicle opened and Maria, the cosmetologist, entered.

"Where are you going, Miss Manchester? The whiteheads . . ."

"My whiteheads and I are going to have to learn to coexist, Maria. I've got an appointment," she fibbed.

Her "appointment" was with the mailman. At one o'clock each afternoon she anxiously awaited his arrival at her parents' house. Though she knew it wasn't right, when she had received that rejection back home in Boston she had immediately re-posted it, with two minor alterations.

Next to sex she had marked *M* instead of *F* and to forestall recognition of her name she had called herself D. Manchester. She was certain that Gary LeBlanc, the leader of the proposed expedition, had not read past that first line on her original application. Gary LeBlanc was a renowned and respected leader whose name she often heard spoken of reverentially in the climbing circles she frequented. Though the world of dedicated climbers was small, she had never met him and had little desire ever to do so. In spite of the fact that climbing teams were usually quite egalitarian, the leader being leader in little more than name, Gary LeBlanc had a reputation of being strong and dominant. Because of that and because of his well-known aversion to women climbers, many of the more liberal climbers of both sexes stayed away from him.

"But let me finish the cleansing!" Maria broke into her thoughts. "At least a little drying lotion to close the pores. And I'll talk to Raymond, the new makeup man. You won't have to wait. He'll fix you up."

"Don't bother. I like this unfixed feeling."

Maria raised her eyebrows. "Oh, no. You cannot go out like this. Your nose, it is shiny. And there is nothing on your face to protect it."

"Maria," Dana said as she pressed a five-dollar bill into her hand, "don't worry. It's not illegal in New York to have a shiny nose." Maria shrugged as she thanked this curious client of hers.

Distracted by thoughts of the mountains, Dana sailed through the reception room, not even noticing the statuesque consultants behind the counters with their perfect faces, perfect makeup, and perfect smiles. Much of her life Dana had sailed like this through roomfuls of people with whom she had little in common. Call her alienated, call her a loner, she mused. Call her by any term that was currently in vogue. What was undeniably true was that Dana rarely fit in. That she was beautiful with her brownish-gold hair, her luminescent gray eyes, her finely sculpted face, and slim figure, made it all the more difficult for people to understand. Why would a woman who looked like that lack for dates? Why would she have so few friends? Why indeed? It was, Dana knew, because she wanted it that way. She was different. She had always known that. Born in the lap of luxury, she was the despair of a well-meaning family. She could have had it all. And she chose to have none of it. She spurned the fur coat for graduation. She refused the imported sports car, buying herself a jeep instead. Naturally athletic, tennis was the one sport she had never learned. In a fit of anger her mother had accused her of spitefulness, saying she didn't play tennis because if she did, then she would have no reason to avoid the country club, with its manicured grass courts. Dana had admitted that her mother had a point. It was just that the women who played at the club indulged in the sport, she suspected, more for the fun of wearing their starched tennis dresses than for the pleasure of batting the ball over the net.

Sprinting down the Georgette Klinger Salon's winding stairway, Dana tried to hail one of Fifth Avenue's passing fleet of cabs. There was a commuter train leaving for Scarsdale in fifteen minutes. If they ran into no traffic jams on the way to Grand Central Station, she would make it. Although she had promised her mother that she would spend the day in the city to do some shopping, for her wardrobe was "frightful," Dana could not bear the thought of going through the racks of designer clothing even, or especially, in the thickly carpeted splendor of

12

stores like Bendel's or Saks. There was nothing more boring to her than shopping. A facial was preferable to that! Her poor mother, Dana mused, to be stuck with such a daughter. Her mother's offspring should have been blond and cute or dark and tailored. Dana was neither. Her favorite mode of dress was jeans and flannel shirt. Her mother did admit, though ruefully, that on Dana, jeans looked better than Nipon did on most other women.

After five minutes of futilely flagging passing taxis (each had been occupied or off-duty), an old-fashioned large yellow cab screeched to a halt in front of her. As she settled into the torn plastic seat, Dana leaned toward the murky partition that separated driver and passenger.

"Grand Central Station, and could you get me there quickly, please? I've got a train to catch."

"Whaddya mean, lady? I'll do my best but if ya want me to step on it, you pay for the ticket. The whole world's got a train to catch, ya know what I mean?"

"Of course," Dana faltered. "I didn't mean . . ."

The cabbie eyed her in the mirror. "You somebody famous? Huh? I mean you look like somebody famous, ya know?"

Dana laughed. "I'm not famous. You're thinking of someone else."

The grizzled man managed to negotiate the midtown traffic with his gaze still fixed on the rearview mirror. "Heck, you're pretty enough to be famous. Tell you what I'll do. I'll get you to your train in time. You ought to be famous, you know?"

Dana smiled. "Thanks. I guess."

Hoping that he would look at the traffic instead of at her, Dana pursed her lips unattractively and studied her knees. Whatever else could be said for that cabbie, that he

13

could drive blindfolded or that he had a taste for natural-looking women, he did get her there on time. For that Dana was truly grateful.

The train ride to Scarsdale was uneventful. Laden with magazines she had bought hastily at the newsstand, she nonetheless stared unseeingly through dust-streaked windows for the entire ride. All she could concentrate on was Gary LeBlanc's expedition.

Under normal circumstances, that is, with a normal leader, Dana would never have made out a formal application to participate in the climb. At her level of expertise teams were usually formed by the process of networking. When she had first heard about the climb, Dana had indeed made some well-placed phone calls asking to be recommended. The unanimous response was "You're nuts. He'll never take you. He hates women," or some variant thereof. Not one of the people she had contacted would even broach the subject with Gary LeBlanc.

"Who's there?" her mother called as Dana slammed the door of the sprawling gray stone colonial in a secluded section of Scarsdale.

"It's me, Mother," Dana called, thinking that this two-week visit with her parents was about one week too long. When she was home she felt no older than twelve and she figured it would feel the same even when she was fifty.

"Back so soon?" the elegantly svelte Mrs. Manchester asked reproachfully as she came to greet her daughter. "Where are the packages? Are you having them delivered? And what happened to your face? Why don't you have makeup on?"

"Any mail?" Dana asked, carefully deciding to ignore the questions.

"Nothing for you, dear. What did you buy? Did you see

14

the new Halston collection? Exquisite. I do hope you bought one of his little numbers. You'd be smashing."

"I didn't go shopping, Mother. Are you sure there's no mail for me?"

"You didn't go shopping! Dana, how could you? We have no less than three affairs next week. What are you going to wear?" Her mother's brow lowered. "Oh," she said, remembering suddenly, "a telegram came for you."

"Where is it?" Dana's voice was sharper than she intended, for she usually bent over backwards to avoid arguing with her mother.

"On the mantelpiece, I think," her mother replied absentmindedly. Running to the den, Dana found the telegram not on the mantelpiece but atop a marble shelf, tucked between two Lladro figurines, porcelain figurines by the Spaniard Juan Lladro, which dotted her mother's house.

"Credentials admirable STOP Interview Wednesday, nineteenth STOP Three P.M. Plaza Hotel New York City STOP." It was signed Gary LeBlanc. Her heart beat wildly, from consternation or happiness she didn't know. Yes, she had a shot at making the team, but when LeBlanc found out that she was an F instead of an M it was going to be a long shot indeed. Yet the man had nerve. Today was the nineteenth. The time was one o'clock and the meeting he had set up was two hours away. No wonder his reputation in mountaineering society was fearsome. With no time to check train schedules, she grabbed her car keys, her down-filled jacket, and nylon shoulder bag. There was nothing like spending a day commuting back and forth between Westchester and Manhattan, she thought.

"'Bye, Mother. Don't wait up for me."

15

"Where are you going?"

"On an interview back in the city. It may take a while."

"I have some people from the club coming to dinner tonight. Didn't I tell you? How unfair you are, Dana. They're only coming to catch a glimpse of you. You're so rarely around anymore."

"I'm sorry, Mother, but this is very important to me."

Mrs. Manchester sucked in her cheeks. "I hope it doesn't have to do with your"—she paused distastefully—"mountains."

Dana pecked her mother's smooth cheek. "I've got to run. I'm late."

"At least put on some lipstick!" her mother called after her. Pulling her canary yellow jeep out of the garage, she turned the ignition. It felt good to be behind the wheel. She and the jeep never saw much of each other when she was in Scarsdale. In Scarsdale she drove one of her parents' two Lincolns. Eccentricity was one thing. Unseemliness another.

Out on the road Dana began to feel as if she were coming alive again. Her parents were fine. She loved them. But after forty-eight hours in the same house, she began to feel that she had entered a time warp. After a week she had begun to feel comatose. It was hard to be you, she mused, when that you was a person your parents neither understood nor wanted to understand. She, with her disdain for conspicuous consumption, or conspicuous achievement, in the form of marriage to someone with an M.D., Esq., D.D.S., or chairmanship of the board, was the antithesis of everything her parents believed in. It was absurd, they maintained, that someone would want to leave a world of wealth and ease for a world of austerity and hazard. Yet how strange that at the age of twenty-eight, a divorcee, and long on her own, her mother should still be telling her to put on lipstick, still trying to change her. Dana smiled to herself. She never wore lipstick. Maybe at the hospital they had gotten mixed up and given her to the wrong set of parents.

With that final thought she switched her musings to the interview ahead which made little beads of perspiration stand out on her upper lip. To be part of this expedition with one of America's finest climbers, in the awesome McKinley setting of wind, sun, and ice would be the ultimate joy for any serious climber, and that was the one thing Dana was certain she was. She had never been more serious about anything in her life. Nothing had ever given her the feeling of completeness, of purity, of accomplishment, that she got from climbing. With nothing else was her mind focused so intently on the task at hand. It was on the mountains that she saw herself and the world with a stunning clarity. It was on the mountains that she found peace.

She slowed down as she hit traffic and was relieved when she finally entered the expressway where the traffic maintained a steady speed of fifty miles an hour. It took her just seventy minutes to make it to the Plaza on Fifty-ninth Street and Central Park South, parking included. It was almost a half mile from here that she had spent her morning in padded solitude at Georgette Klinger. Maria would positively yelp, Dana thought wryly, if she could see her skin now, dusty and dry from the cold wind that had been hitting it for the past hour. The window on the driver's side of her jeep didn't close all the way. It was something Dana had been meaning to get repaired.

Throwing her shoulders back, she tucked her shirt neatly into her pants before entering the deluxe hotel, not caring that she was early.

"Will you ring Mr. LeBlanc's room, please?" she asked the clerk behind the hotel register. "Tell him that, uh, Manchester is here to see him."

"Yes, ma'am." The clerk complied willingly. He gazed covertly at Dana as he rang the room. Working in a major New York hotel, he was accustomed to beautiful women. Naturally beautiful women were still a relatively rare phenomenon however.

"He'll meet you in the Oak Bar," the clerk informed her. "He said in ten minutes."

The Oak Bar, so named for its oak bar, oak tables, and oak paneling, was tastefully understated, its main feature being the magnificent paintings of Fifth Avenue in the rain, the Plaza, and the park, that covered three of its walls. Because it was past the lunch hour and too early for cocktails, there was only a scattering of patrons. With the exception of one woman in a tight red jersey dress with a plunging neckline, they were all men.

Taking a seat at the far corner of the bar, she ordered a Heineken and prayed that when Gary LeBlanc arrived she would not appear as nervous as she felt. Her prayers were not answered.

She knew immediately it was he when a tall, olive-skinned, hulking form in Outlander khaki and flannel appeared at the entrance. His hair was a shiny black, his eyes, even from across the room, shone with an intelligent light, his demeanor as he gazed at the bar's occupants was one of calm command. He seemed to be all muscle and sinewy strength with skin that stretched taut over prominent cheekbones and a firm jaw. There was nothing slack about this man.

18

The woman in the red dress saw him at the same time as Dana did. Sliding off her stool, she sashayed over to him. Dana watched, flabbergasted, as he smiled at the woman's words. The great LeBlanc, the Balboa, the Gandhi of the mountains! Iron will, unshakable discipline —that was the party line when it came to Gary LeBlanc. What would people say if they knew that like a conventioneer in a three-piece polyester suit, he, too, was an easy mark for a good-looking professional? Disgusted, Dana turned away, knocking her beer on her lap in the process. Jumping up as the cold brew seeped through the knees of her corduroys, she uttered soft deprecations. The bartender was at her side with a fistful of napkins for which she thanked him profusely.

Stealing a glance at the doorway, she was relieved to find that the woman was pouting as she flounced away and was gently expelled by the bartender. At least he didn't mix business with pleasure, if that's what it could be called. This was, after all, a business meeting he had arranged. Without warning their eyes met over the wad of soggy paper she was about to lay on the counter. Dana drew in her breath. This man was too handsome. He averted his glance. When Dana looked at him again he was watching the door in puzzlement, probably thinking that Dana Manchester had not yet arrived in the bar. She squared her shoulders as she went to greet him while wondering at his reaction when he learned that Dana Manchester was a woman.

"Hi." She smiled jauntily.

He cleared his throat, a look of astonishment playing in his eyes. "No, thank you, miss. I'm sorry."

She noticed a bright red flush starting at his neck. It was

her turn to look astonished as the import of his words dawned on her.

"You think I'm . . ." She gestured haphazardly with her index finger from him to herself. "I'm a . . ." She laughed suddenly, too surprised to be angry. She had been taken for many things in her life—weird, strange, aloof—but never had she been taken for a prostitute. "I'm not wearing fishnet stockings, you know. I wasn't aware that corduroys were part of the uniform. Are you Gary LeBlanc?"

A sick expression came over his face. "That's right. Who are you?"

"Dana Manchester. I received your telegram and," she giggled, "here I am. Ready to solicit"—she paused mischievously—"a place on your team." For the life of her she couldn't tell why she was in such a good mood. A more inauspicious beginning for the most important interview of her life could not have been imagined.

"Dana Manchester." He repeated her name lugubriously, as if it were his death sentence. He closed his eyes briefly. "How can I apologize? I don't know what to say." He shook his head. Enjoying his discomfiture, Dana leveled a cool glance at him and said nothing. "I thought . . . I mean, you don't look it. It was just that coming over to me after that other one . . ."

"Other one?"

"That other woman," he explained, confused.

"I imagine it must be difficult trying to distinguish among the females of the species," she remarked throatily.

"I thought you were a man," he said finally.

Throwing back her head, she laughed that curiously infectious laugh that made people immediately want to become her friend. "First you think I'm a lady of the night. Then you think I'm a man. Either I have an identity problem or you need glasses!"

His mouth twisted derisively. "All right. You've had your fun. Can't say I blame you though." He put a hand lightly on her elbow. "Come on, Dana Manchester. Let's find a table and talk."

While he ordered the drinks Dana studied Gary Le-Blanc. From up close the impression of solidity and power, of competence and confidence, was overshadowed by his dark brown eyes that seemed fathomless. She had never seen eyes that so expressed and defined a person.

"When do you do your climbing, on weekends and vacations?" he asked, turning his attention back to her. "My expedition will take weeks of preparation. How would you be able to get away from the job I presume you have?"

"You shouldn't presume anything," she answered with a grin. "I'm a guide for a couple of mountaineering clubs, and I do office temp work in between. It's good for the soul. It reminds me how much of a non-office person I am. After a couple of weeks behind a desk I start getting itchy all over."

He laughed. "I can relate to that. But do those little jobs leave you with enough money to stake yourself on climbs?"

She blushed. "Well, there's also a trust fund. I hardly ever touch it, except if there's an emergency. When you've dropped a bottle of hand cream down your toilet and it won't flush anymore, it's hard to stand on principle." Dana couldn't tell whether he was about to chuckle or frown.

He frowned. "You've got a trust fund *and* principles?"

Dana glared. What did he know? Let it pass, she told herself, if you want to go on this expedition.

"The Plaza's a nice contrast to climbing," he said in a neutral tone.

Nodding her agreement, Dana asked in as pleasant a voice as she could muster, "What brings you here? You live in New England, don't you?"

"I used to. I live in Alaska now, near Fairbanks. How about you? If I remember correctly, your application gave a Boston address for residence and Scarsdale for temporary address. You visiting folks?"

"That's right. I'll be going home in a week."

"I'll be up north myself then, visiting the old stomping grounds. Meanwhile, I've got business here in New York. I figured it was a good time to get some interviewing done also. Quite a few of you New Yorkers think you want a crack at the Karstens Ridge." He laughed as if at a funny joke. "Yep," he said, "my next interview is probably with a seventy-four-year-old lady who drives a moped in midtown."

"Or with some jerk who thinks just because she's been climbing religiously for five years and has done Rainier, Pinnacle Gully, and Dracula she can take on McKinley." She affected a laugh and shook her head. "Some people are just crazy, I guess."

She folded her arms across her chest, secure in the knowledge that he was impressed. Pinnacle Gully in Huntington Ravine in New Hampshire simulated parts of the planet's most difficult climbs. What made it so hard was not only the technical aspect of it. It was, in winter, an ice climb of five or six hundred feet which, for sheer ice climbing, is exhaustingly high. It was Dracula, though, in the Frankenstein Cliffs which was her greatest accom-

22

plishment. Most of it is a ninety-degree vertical, but at the top there is an overhang so that one had to climb upside down, like an ant crawling on the ceiling, in order to go over the top.

Narrowing his brown eyes, Gary LeBlanc looked at her suspiciously. "That was on your application, wasn't it? *You* did those climbs?" His voice was incredulous.

"One doesn't generally fudge on applications to join climbing expeditions. I realize that honesty on job applications is fast becoming a relic of the past, but even someone of the fair sex has to realize that claiming to have done Dracula is not exactly like claiming to have been in the secretarial pool for two years when it was only for two weeks."

He hesitated. "I didn't mean to imply that you had lied about your experience on your application."

"Oh, didn't you?" she asked with a little smile. In some perverse way, she was enjoying this encounter. That she had this indomitable big lunk on the run was clear beyond a shadow of a doubt.

"It was just that you took me by surprise." He flashed her a smile that could melt ice. "First, by being a woman, after marking M on your application. A rather gutsy ploy, by the way. Second, by being a beautiful woman. Third, by being a beautiful woman mountain climber."

"Is that three strikes and I'm out?" she asked with a coquettish grin.

"No."

"But I hear you hate women," she blurted out with what she hoped was disarming ingenuousness.

His eyes raked lecherously over her body. "Women are great," he said with a smile.

"I'm talking about on a climb," she stated acerbically.

"And I'm talking about in bed." He lowered his voice seductively. "Or even in a sleeping bag. But not on a climb."

She bristled. "That's an awful thing to say. You sound positively prehistoric."

"What's wrong with that? Neanderthal man did all right for himself. Maybe even did some climbing."

"Why don't you write a book," she asked sarcastically, *"Sex and Climbing Among Neanderthal Men."*

"I think I'll stick to sex and the contemporary mountain climber," he laughed. "But not on a mountain."

"I wish I had brought a tape recorder with me," she said hotly. "You'd be embarrassed, I hope, if your sentiments on these matters ever became known in climbing circles." She paused. "But I think we've had enough of this pleasant banter. It's time to talk business."

"I have been," he countered blandly, "and, besides, my sentiments on these matters are known."

She frowned severely. "You asked me on this interview because, presumably, something in my resume impressed you. I want to talk about that, and I want to talk about the Karstens Ridge. I also want to talk about you. I wouldn't entrust my life to someone who, for example, liked to play Russian roulette." Dana sucked in her breath. For all her nervous tremors before meeting him, it looked like she was in control of this interview.

"For the record, I don't even play pinochle," he cut in. "But anyway, it's out of the question. There's no way you're coming along."

"Why not?"

"You wouldn't be able to make it, and your being there would endanger the rest of us."

The rage that welled up inside her threatened to spill

out. Dana counted to ten, a trick which never worked. She was saved by the arrival of the waitress with a tray of crackers and cheese, a Jack Daniel's for Gary and another Heineken for her.

"Male chauvinist bozos like you ought to be in jail." She smiled lightly to show she was kidding. Her attempt at humor, however, did little to assuage her anger. "Since that's highly unlikely, I may as well tell you that bringing you into court on discrimination charges is a bit more probable." She drummed her fingers on the tabletop. "I have always been an asset on every climb. Nobody's life has been endangered because of me." She narrowed her eyes mockingly. "There's only one life that's going to be endangered, and I'll let you guess whose that is."

"I consider myself duly warned." He leaned forward casually. "What method of execution are you planning on using? I already feel myself pierced by the daggers in your eyes. But before you do the dirty deed, answer one question. What's a sophisticated woman like you . . ."

"Don't say it!" She groaned. "I'll tell you. I'm the sole support of a sick, old mother and the only happiness I can give her is by planting her black and rose silk scarf on top of Mount McKinley and letting it fly over the world as her banner." Their eyes met and they laughed.

"Well, you don't *look* like a mountain climber," he finished lamely.

"You don't look like a . . . a guy who wears baggy underwear," she giggled.

"I take it that guys who wear baggy underwear are classic male chauvinist pigs?"

"If you want to put it that way," she assented with the merest quirk of an eyebrow.

By all rights, she mused, she ought to be nursing her

hostility. Instead, she was joking with this person as if he were her dinner date. No wonder her family couldn't understand her. She couldn't understand herself. She caught Gary LeBlanc studying her.

"You're really serious about climbing, aren't you?"

She nodded. "It's the only thing I've ever been serious about." Her tone was sheepish. "I don't know how good that is, but it's true."

"Are you married?"

"Why?" she queried. "Do you want to know whom to send the body to?"

"I'm curious."

"Well"—she blew out her breath—"I was married once. But my former husband couldn't understand why I didn't bleach my hair blond and spend my life learning new recipes. So the comedy ended—*finita la commedia*, as they say in *italiano*."

"You sound bitter," Gary said quietly.

"Not at all. I was glad when it was over. It's just that for my whole life people wanted me to be a certain way. I am what I am."

"So you climb mountains to show the world how different you are," he concluded.

She felt a hot flush starting on her cheeks. "I climb mountains because that's what I love doing. There's no need to psychoanalyze me. It's very simple. I'm never more me than when I'm driving in a piton or belaying."

"At least you use the terms well," he teased, referring to her mention of pitons, the special nails that climbers hammer into the cracks and fissures of rock, and to belaying, a common method of climbing with ropes.

"I use the tools well," she corrected him. "I've only been climbing for five years, Gary, but I'm talented."

26

He sat back in his chair without saying anything. He held his hands in front of him, the fingers of one hand touching the corresponding fingers of the other. "It's impossible," he said finally. "Even if you could do it, which I doubt, a woman on such a climb would be a distraction. On this expedition we need absolute concentration, absolute calm. A tight little derriere before our eyes could mean the breaking of focus, a resultant tragedy."

"Ho-ho," she mocked him. "And make sure we don't elect a woman for president, or if we do, she had better have lots of cellulite you know where. Or else the wrong people might become distracted and press the naughty buttons by mistake and the whole world might blow up. So down with tight little derrieres! And by the way, how do you know what kind I have?" The twinkle in her eyes was mischievous.

"I have a good imagination," he answered dryly. Without looking at her he opened the manila envelope he had carried into the bar. From it he retrieved her application, which he quickly perused.

"You've got a hell of a background in climbing," he admitted. "I don't know. It's against my better judgment but, uh, maybe I should give the matter some more thought."

"How much more thought do you have to give it?" she asked impatiently.

Annoyance flashed across his sharp features. "Why is it so important for you to come on this expedition?"

"Because it's what I've been striving for these past five years. I have a feeling it's no less important for me than for you. You have a dream, and, sorry to say, this lowly tight-derriered female seems to be sharing it."

"You have a charming way of putting things," he

chuckled as he signaled the waitress for a refill. "Do you want anything?"

Shaking her head, she indicated her half-full stein. She looked down at the brew. Maybe she ought to forget this expedition. There would be others. But he was the best. And if you were going to climb North America's most challenging trail, you ought to go with the best.

"I want to go with you," she said quietly. Conviction shone in her eyes. "You won't find anyone better. Maybe I'm not as strong as you, but I can tie every knot there is in a couple of seconds with my eyes closed. I'm light on my feet, I have a superb sense of balance, and excellent judgment. I have the stamina to make a marathon runner envious, and patience that might have been learned with an Indian guru."

He heaved a long sigh. "I climbed with two women once. I swore I would never do that again. Not only couldn't they share the load, they complained constantly. I would never have thought it. These were women who looked like Russian cosmonauts. You look like a cover girl."

"There's a Sherpa locked inside this deceptively, uh . . ."

"Gorgeous," he supplied.

"Gorgeous," she laughed, "body."

"I hope it's a Sherpa," he said soberly, "because if by some fluke you did get yourself on my team, you'd have to have some Himalayan blood in you. The Karstens Ridge is the closest climb in the continental United States to Mount Everest."

"I hope you're not forgetting the all-woman team that climbed Everest a few years back," she retorted smugly.

"No female climber would let me forget that," he said with a crestfallen grin.

"Well?" she asked.

"Well, what?"

"Are you going to take me?"

"Hey!" he protested. "I've got half a dozen more people to interview. How can you expect an answer just like that?" He snapped his fingers.

"You could at least tell me whether you're going to do an endurance climb with me."

Dana knew that if she had any chance at all, it would only be if he saw her doing what she did best. And she knew that unless he agreed to take her on a trial climb he would be having a drink with her and that would be the end of it. If people were to do a serious climb together, they first had to know if they were compatible climbers. Some of the best stock trails, such as Pinnacle Gully and Dracula, could be found in New England. Technically they were as difficult as Karstens Ridge, but were much safer, most of them being fifty feet or so high.

A slow grin broke out over his face. "I've got one spot left on my team. The other two are filled with men who are so anti-woman they make me look like a feminist. But I'll tell you what. I won't even interview the other candidates, for their experience is more limited than yours, if, and it's a big if, if you can pass my test."

"Great!" she exploded. "Alaska, here I come!"

"Not so fast," he cautioned. "You've done Pinnacle Gully. You've done Dracula. Those are two impressive feats. But New England has another trail I'd like to see you do. Scale it with me, and I welcome you to the McKinley expedition."

Jokingly, she rose from her chair. "See you. I'm going to buy a new pair of climbing shoes now."

"Calm down," he ordered, "you haven't heard what it is."

"What does it matter?" she tossed back. "I can do it." She laughed giddily. "I knew there was a teddy bear behind that gruff exterior!"

An emotion she couldn't put her finger on flashed across his eyes. It was a mixture of guilt, amusement, and hunger; and it made goose bumps stand up on her arms.

He looked at her steadily. "It's the Black Dike."

Uncomprehendingly it seemed, she heard the words. Without moving, without looking at him, she felt her spirits sink. She had been set up. This was a way of avoiding ethical or personal conflicts by pretending to give her a chance to compete for a place with him. Black Dike in Cannon Cliffs, Franconia Notch, New Hampshire, was classified a five, the most difficult grade, by the Appalachian Mountain Club. She had heard talk about it but had never known anybody, nor known anybody who had known anybody, who had ever even attempted Black Dike. In a gentle ski area there was a tame ski run with lodge, lifts, and easy trails at Cannon Mountain. If you took the lift to the top of Cannon Mountain and stood there looking behind you, there would be a startling sight. It would look like half the mountain were missing, as if someone had sliced it off and carried it away. You would be staring down a sheer wall of six hundred feet through the middle of which ran a scar. In the winter that scar gets filled in with ice, becoming a six-hundred-foot icicle. That icicle is Black Dike. There were probably no more than fifty North American climbers who had ever climbed it.

What a miserable man he was to bring her so high so

30

she could crash so low! Dana felt tears rim her eyes. Oh, great, she thought, she was going to cry! Well, she wouldn't give him the satisfaction. Holding her breath till it hurt, she fought to control herself.

"When," she whispered, "shall we do the Dike?"

It was a second before he answered. "One week from today will give us enough time to get our equipment together."

"One week from today," she echoed. "I'll be ready." If it kills me, she thought wretchedly. And it just might!

CHAPTER TWO

Touch, sit, twist, claw. Touch, sit, twist, claw. Dana lay back on her exercise mat pushing the small of her back hard against the floor. Her one hundred sit-ups finished, she started on one hundred jumping jacks. Even to the tune of a Willie Nelson song, jumping jacks were a colossal bore, she mused. Nonetheless, she persevered, following with push-ups, somersaults, and running in place.

Every fifteen minutes or so, she noticed out of the corner of her eye a baleful Mrs. Manchester peeking in. After an hour her mother could no longer hold her tongue.

"The delivery boy came, dear. There are ten dresses on your bed waiting to be tried on."

Slowing to a walk, Dana grinned indulgently. "All right, Mother. Just give me a chance to shower."

"Your father and I are going out now. A luncheon at the club for the McClean girl's engagement. We should be home for dinner. Will you be here?"

"I don't know. I guess so. Have a good time and, yes,

I promise, I'll like at least three of the dresses," she said, anticipating her mother's next words.

Serenity graced her mother's visage as she departed. Dana smiled to herself. It was very easy to gladden her mother's heart. She really ought to make more of an effort, at least when she was visiting, which wasn't all that often. All she had to do was pretend an interest in clothes and in the eligible men that were incessantly paraded in front of her. That wasn't the most difficult of tasks. She would, she promised herself, be a better daughter. She would take at least three of the dresses, no matter how flouncy or fluffy. Her mother's taste being what it was, frills were a sure bet. No matter. She could always give them to Goodwill later on.

After her shower she stood in front of the mirror pulling a comb through her damp hair. Twisting it in a knot on top of her head, she was oblivious to the effect it had on her face. Without the distraction of hair, the delicate perfection of her features gave her an angelic, almost otherworldly appearance. Brushing on a touch of blusher and a thin coat of lipstick, she slipped into a pair of gold, high-heeled sandals. If she was going to try on these creations, she might as well do it right.

She grimaced. The first, a tight, lavender number in satin with tiers of ruffles at the bottom made her look like a can-can dancer. The second, in red with handsewn beads, made her feel like a flamenco dancer, and the third, a delicate white eyelet, as if she were going to her junior prom. The fourth, fifth, and sixth were variations on a theme. The seventh dress, an almost militarily simple navy silk with padded shoulders and a decolletage that plunged to her navel, necessitating the removal of her bra, she actually liked. No, she thought, as she pirouetted in front of the mirror. She adored it. It could, however, be improved with accessories. Rummaging through her jewelry box, she found a choker of three twisted strands of pearls and matching earrings, which she clipped on. She surveyed her elegant reflection in the mirror. Just then she heard the doorbell ring.

Not more dresses! she thought with a sinking sensation as she recalled her mother's propensity for buying outfits by the score.

"Hi."

"You're not a messenger," she intoned dully.

Holding out his lumberjacketed arms, Gary turned the wrists over. "No gold braid here. Hmm," he observed his zipper. "Brass buttons seem to be missing. Can't be a singing messenger. Baritone's missing too." He opened his mouth wide and attempted in a cacophonously off-key voice to sing, "If this is Dana Manchester the mountaineer, I trust her climbing togs are not what I see here."

Closing her eyes, Dana sighed a deep, "Oh, no." When she opened them, it was upon a Gary LeBlanc who was gazing with more than passing interest at the creamy twin globes of her partially exposed breasts. She stifled an urge to fold her arms over her chest, which would have been even more embarrassing. But it wasn't only embarrassment that she felt. It was pride, for she took pleasure in her allure for Gary and it was titillating. If this were another life, she could imagine that the way he was looking at her now would be but a prelude to a night of mad and frenzied lovemaking. As skilled a climber, as sharp-tongued as she was, she became acutely aware of the discordance between them—of her delicate bones and her lush curves, of his bigness, his hardness, his lean, straight lines. She became aware of the desire in his eyes when he

34

raised them to hers and she knew that she wanted him to crush her against him.

"Of thee I sing," he crooned.

"Of thee I am not amused," she said acerbically. "Couldn't you have called first?"

"Well," he drawled, "I just happened to be in the neighborhood. . . ."

"You just happened to be on Harvest Drive in Scarsdale when you're staying at the Plaza on Fifty-ninth Street and Central Park South? Quite a coincidence!"

"Actually," he laughed as he swung his rucksack from his shoulders, "I wanted to show you some new equipment I bought for the Black Dike. I've got a rented car and, well, a few days in Manhattan and I was beginning to forget what fresh air smells like so . . . Hell, what am I doing? I don't have to explain." He looked at her with calm assurance. "Don't I get invited in?"

She moved aside. "Come in, of course."

"Nice place," Gary remarked as he looked around the marble-tiled foyer. "Do I get introduced to your family, or do I first have to get a Dun and Bradstreet rating?"

"My mother's parrots are the only ones home. I'm sure they'll be glad to meet you. You can caw at each other. You'll get along just fine."

Gary seated himself in a gray velvet chair. "You been getting ready for the climb?"

"Sure. I've been touching my toes a couple of times a day," she said flippantly. "I didn't want to tear any silk stockings, you know." She paced nervously in front of him. "Do you want a drink or something?" Without waiting for an answer she went to the wall where she pressed a button, causing the panels to slide away to expose a fully stocked bar. "Jack Daniel's?"

35

"Milk."

"Milk?"

"Chocolate milk if you have it."

She pressed the button to close the panels. "Why don't you help yourself? The kitchen's that way." She pointed. "I'll be right down. I want to change."

"Slipping into something more comfortable?" he teased. "You couldn't get a hell of a lot more comfortable than that." The insinuation was plain.

"Glad you approve," she tossed over her shoulder as she ran upstairs. Her fingers were slippery as she tried to unclasp the pearls, only managing with her third attempt. She pulled off the earrings, tossed the dress on her bed, and searched for her jeans. Just as she found them she paused, her eye spying the new lavender pants outfit in sweat shirt material that her mother had also had sent over. The casual material did nothing to hide the designer chic that fairly shouted through the soft lines of the outfit. If he thought of her as a rich, materialistic snob, she might as well give him some fuel with which to feed his prejudices. The outfit heightened the deep gray of her eyes and emphasized the smooth ivory quality of her skin. It looked as if it were designed with her in mind. She uncoiled her hair and brushed it so that it hung straight and shiny to the middle of her back. The image that stared back at her from the mirror bore little resemblance to the unadorned, careless way in which she pictured herself. She was satisfied.

When she returned downstairs Gary was kneeling in front of his rucksack carefully emptying it of its contents. An empty glass with a dark chocolate ring on the bottom stood on the coffee table.

"I see you found the milk."

"Yep," he answered without turning around. "Take a look here. What do you think?"

Kneeling beside him, Dana picked up several pitons. She examined them intently, turning them over, running her fingers along their edges, testing the points. In the cold steel of the equipment she sensed adventure and found herself momentarily transported to distant peaks.

Her brow was furrowed when finally she spoke. "This wart-hog piton is fine, a new model, I see. And I like the Austrian pitons and the tubular ice screws. Maybe, just to be on the safe side we ought to bring along half-tube pitons in case we run into some soft ice. I know it's unlikely with the weather the way it's been this winter in New Hampshire, but with conditions of ice being so unstable, it might be a smart thing to do."

Still on his knees, Gary turned to look at her. She read amazement and respect in his eyes. The mixture annoyed her. Despite her resume, he still didn't quite believe in her expertise.

Withdrawing a scratch pad from his pocket, he wrote, "Half-tube pitons." Next he took out an ice hammer for her inspection and then different models of crampons, the sharp spikes mounted on metal frames which when strapped to climbing boots provide traction on snow and ice.

"I prefer neoprene to nylon or cloth," she said crisply as she pulled and twisted the different straps used for attaching crampons to boots. "And I like these nickel-plated buckles rather than the sliding fasteners."

"My choice precisely," he agreed. "I'm glad to see we agree on hardware. I hope that's not all we agree on," he added with a grin.

"I like chocolate milk too," she said shrilly. "That

makes two things. What I don't like are opinionated boors or judgmental people."

"Perhaps we should confine our conversations to climbing," he said evenly.

"Perhaps."

"The equipment is expensive, but I imagine you won't want to discuss that. Money is no object, I'm sure," he said.

"I don't mind discussing money," she rejoined. "It's you, not I, who seems to be hung up on it. Of course, that's understandable. To one so spiritual and pure as you, how hopelessly crass we, from the hinterlands of Gucci and Pucci, must appear. You, naturally, finance yourself with idealism."

"My money is earned. I work for it."

His words stung. She felt the blood draining from her face. She supposed this was what was meant by being caught between the devil and the deep blue sea. To her family she was practically considered a hobo and to Gary LeBlanc she was one of the idle rich.

"Excuse me," she said acidly. "I never learned to be anything other than a parasite. I'm the product of my environment." She would never let him know, she resolved, of the annual dividends from her trust fund that she usually turned over intact to one of her favorite charities, usually some environmental cause. And he would never know of the many soup and sandwich dinners she ate when there were no climbing parties to lead and when temporary jobs were scarce. She would never tell him that she, too, found inherited money to be an embarrassment. She was glad her parents were wealthy. Her father had earned it. But other than being born, she herself had done nothing for the money that so easily came her way. It wasn't that she had anything against wealth. If she had done something to deserve it, she might have enjoyed it. But she hadn't. And she chose not to, for although she saw the pleasures that wealth could bring, she had not dedicated her life to acquiring that wealth. It would be too easy, then, to miss out on life's truest pleasures—the smell of new grass, the first sighting of a majestic blue ridge, mountain peaks, the graceful soaring of an eagle in flight. No amount of money could buy her the freedom she sought. That freedom was a gift she had given herself.

Entirely missing the facetiousness of her statement, he answered dryly, "Product of your environment. That's the same excuse every criminal from here to San Quentin uses. You're only what you want to be."

"Rather sanctimonious aren't you, Dr. Albert Schweitzer? Not everybody chooses to be so self-sacrificing, however. I've chosen the life of a social butterfly, and as soon as we finish here with carabiners and harnesses and the rest of the equipment, I'm going to a fashion show where I shall proceed to spend thousands of dollars on frocks and baubles which I'll probably wear once," she lied.

Abruptly changing his mood, Gary chuckled, "You're as ornamental as the prettiest of those baubles, I'll wager."

"And as useless?" she questioned sharply.

"I could think of some use to put you to," he murmured.

Biting back a sharp retort, she drew a deep breath. "Anything else you want me to look at?"

"Me. Look at me."

His hand was on her chin, tilting her head back so that her eyes met his. As before, she had the same dizzying sensation of drowning in the deep, velvety depths of his eyes. She was immobile as his face swam before her, as his mouth, full and sharply defined, closed in on her.

"Gary . . ."

And then his mouth was on hers, silencing her, claiming her in a tender kiss. His lips, his teeth, his tongue, were hot, moist, demanding. His fingers moved sensuously along the curve of her jaw, sliding down to caress her throat and shoulders. Raking his hands through her hair, he made the rich locks fall with wild abandon over her eyes and across her forehead.

No, the rational part of her mind screamed. Don't be a fool.

She felt the strong ripples of muscle in his broad chest, in his steel-like arms, in his long legs, as he insinuated his body against her. She fought against a raging desire to wrap her arms around him, though she felt her lips opening slightly to receive him, as if it were the most natural thing in the world. And as he took advantage of those parted lips, she felt his kiss searing through her, as though she had never felt another's embrace. She felt it in her mouth, her abdomen, in the quickening of her heartbeat, in the tautening of her nipples, in an almost-forgotten tugging in her womb, in a weakening of her knees. His mouth searched deeply inside hers, bringing her, like a fall from a sheer cliff, close to a point of no return. When he groaned she heard it as a primitive sound of male desire, and she answered with a gasping sound of her own.

Her mind cleared. Taking a long breath, she placed both hands squarely against the hard wall of his chest and pushed. The ease with which he let her go and the gentleness which she saw in his eyes left her flustered. Her hand in midair trembled slightly.

"I want to be your lover," he said huskily.

His words, prosaic words, nonetheless suffused her with warmth and desire. Confused by these emotions so clearly contrary to her best interests, she remained silent.

"We would be good together," he urged. "I think you want me too."

Hugging her arms tightly across her chest, she turned away. Inexplicably a small gathering of tears rimmed her eyelids. He was right. She had wanted him. And it had been a long time since she had felt flames of desire raging, and never so furiously. For that's what it was—pure, unadulterated lust, nothing more. The attraction was intense, but Dana knew about things like that. There was attraction, there was sex, and then there was emptiness. After her divorce she had, in the throes of post-separation depression, engaged in a few meaningless encounters. They had left her more unhappy than she had thought possible. Though it meant she was considered by most of the men she met after that to be old-fashioned, a prude, or frigid, she had kept to her decision to shun sex without love. It had not been a difficult resolution to keep, for she had never been an easy mark for handsome faces and smooth lines. She had always wanted something more. She had never found it. Not even when she was married. Or especially when she was married. Her former husband, shallow and selfish, had never awakened the woman locked inside his wife.

To her former husband Dana had been little more than an acquisition. He was the type of man who had little use for women. A man's man they called him. Twenty-one years old on the day of her wedding, she remembered vividly her hesitation about that marriage even at the moment she stood before the altar. Jeffrey had been ideal for her. Everyone said so. A plastic surgeon, he wor-

41

shipped the ground she walked on. Or rather, she learned quickly, the face she had been born with. Little heed was paid to her ideas, her opinions, her wishes. He scoffed at her love of the outdoors. The sun, he warned, would ruin her complexion. When Dana realized the terrible mistake she had made, she thought seriously about her alternatives. Despite national statistics, she was not the divorcing type. She wanted to make her marriage work. And so, for four long years, Dana dutifully went to the beauty parlor twice a week and wore high heels to the supermarket. The time they spent relating to each other was mostly in the bedroom, and it was there that Dana decided, finally and irrevocably, that there had to be more to life.

Now here was Gary LeBlanc, again a man who made no bones about the contempt in which he held her and her perceived life-style, who with no more than a kiss had started a conflagration that threatened to explode. He was the man who held the key to what she thought she wanted most, to make the greatest climb of her life. She would not, could not, permit naked lust to wreak havoc with her dream and with her soul.

"I want to be on your team, Gary. That's all I want from you."

"We could make a good team," he drawled, his mouth crooking at the corner.

"Don't twist my meaning," she snapped. "You know what I'm talking about. If you're not serious about me as a climber, then you're wasting my time."

"Phew," he whistled through his teeth. "You could have fooled me. Your body and your mouth don't speak the same language."

Dana cringed. She bit her bottom lip. "It's you and I who don't speak the same language. Yours is colored by

42

preconceptions." She paused. "I may have been born with a silver spoon in my mouth, but I wasn't born an idiot. Why don't you gather up your *samples*"—she emphasized the word sarcastically—"and go about your business. I'm sure you have some genuine interviewing to conduct. Unless, of course, you already have your fourth member."

Exasperation was written on his face. "What are you talking about?"

"What I'm talking about is your technique, and not your belaying technique. As a masher you come close to first class—as the most obvious, as the least subtle, as . . ." She hesitated, overcome by indignation. Startled, she heard him laughing.

"So, you think all of this was a pose, the interview, the equipment. All I wanted was to get you in the sack, eh? I certainly did go to a lot of trouble to set you up. Well!" There was a glint of amusement in his eyes. "I'm glad to know you have such a good opinion of yourself. It's important for an expeditionary climber to have self-confidence."

Open-mouthed but with heavy-lidded eyes, she looked at him. The wariness was not yet gone.

His tone was casual as he continued talking. "By the way, I don't manipulate women. I never had to and I don't intend to start now. You either want it, babe, or you don't. Either way it's all right by me. Another thing, if you're going to be climbing with me, you ought to know what kind of a guy I am. I'm honest. Now"—his tone became businesslike—"I have a weather chart I made here. It's looking good in New Hampshire. I don't think we ought to have any problem with the ice delaminating."

Dana nodded. She knew that delamination, the process of the ice coming off in sheets when, for example, a piton was hammered in, was one of the most dangerous risks of ice climbing. If the weather was very cold, the ice would adhere firmly to the underlying rock and the probability of delamination would be minimized.

While she listened with only half an ear to his weather statistics, Dana reflected on the events of a few moments earlier. She flushed. There was no getting away from it. Her dominant mood was not of anger. It was one of self-consciousness. This famous mountaineer was proving a master at the art of embarrassing one Dana Manchester, whether or not that was his intention.

You either want it, babe, or you don't. The cavalier words reverberated in her mind. That was putting it in the proper light, she thought cynically. To him it would have been no more and no less than a physical encounter, probably like climbing a small cliff. She looked down.

"You're not listening," he accused her.

"Sorry," she mumbled as she looked up.

"Is something the matter?"

She disregarded the flash of concern she saw in his eyes. "Not at all. Why should anything be wrong? You come here unannounced, insult me, practically assault me, act as if that were the most natural thing in the world, start talking about the weather, and then you have the gall to ask if anything is the matter? One of us is out of touch with reality!"

Gary looked as if he had been slapped in the face. "I didn't intend to insult you." He paused. "Maybe I did. But you weren't exactly reciting nursery rhymes yourself. As for assaulting you, that's a bit of an exaggeration. To my knowledge a kiss is a kiss, not an assault. Aw, Dana . . ." He passed his hand through his hair. "Loosen up. I

44

wanted to have sex with you. No matter what you say, I think you wanted to have it too."

"I don't *have* sex," she bit out the words. "I *have* lunch, I *have* dates, I *have* arguments, I *have* fun. I even *have* headaches or the flu. But I don't *have* sex. *I* make love."

Gary laughed. "You do *have* a sense of humor. And you *are* righteously indignant. Do you accept my apology? And the assertion that I have more class than I just let on?"

"Whether you do or not is moot. All that concerns me is how you are as a leader and whether or not you agree to have me along. Right now, though, I'm not positive I want to go along. You might get on my nerves."

"I won't get on your nerves. But Joe Flynn and Bill Lewis, the other team members, will. I guarantee it."

"Are you trying to warn me off?" she asked suspiciously. She walked toward the bay window, where she stood facing a winter backyard of bare trees and brown-tinged grass. She sensed rather than heard or saw him following her.

"No," he said gently. "You can take care of yourself. I'm the one who should be on the alert. You're a dangerous woman."

She whirled around to find him mere inches away. Stepping backward, she felt the window ledge jam into her back. "Why do you insist on talking like this? Let's keep our relationship professional." She restrained herself from pushing him away again. The nearness, the scent of him, a musky male odor mingled with spicy aftershave, overwhelmed her, making her feel, even more than when she was three miles above sea level, that she could get no air into her lungs. "Tell me about Flynn and Lewis."

"They're fine mountaineers with a wealth of experience

between them. Veterans. They know Rainier like the backs of their hands, have done some climbing in the French Alps, a little bit in the Chilean Andes and Bill Lewis attempted Annapurna once."

"Impressive," Dana said tightly, trying to smile but feeling for the first time that maybe she was out of her league. "And what's wrong with them?"

"Nothing's wrong with them." He narrowed his eyes, causing the lines etched by wind and sun to stand out against his bronzed complexion.

"Then they won't get on my nerves," she pronounced with a confidence she didn't feel.

"Assuming you actually get to meet them," he said. "You haven't climbed the Black Dike yet."

"I will," she answered calmly, thinking that if she ever quit climbing, she ought to take up acting. "And when I do, they won't get on my nerves."

"Say it enough and you might start believing it," he grinned. "I'll tell you one thing though. They won't like you."

"Oh?"

"They'll have the same reservations about you that I have, only more," he explained.

Dana felt the blood pounding in her temples. "And what about the reservations I have about them? And about you, for that matter? In case nobody ever told you before, there's more to climbing than skill and courage. Otherwise I'd be climbing with monkeys. It takes a certain personality. It takes dependability, trustworthiness, security, and an ability to get along with people under the most trying of circumstances. You don't know how to get along under the *least* trying of circumstances!"

"Circumstances are in the eye of the beholder," he

countered. "To some a mansion in Scarsdale might prove more trying than a barren, snowy peak."

Her voice rose defensively. "I wish you'd get off that soapbox. I do admire your willpower though. You must be suffering terribly at the luxurious Plaza. Next time you come to New York I'll get you a reservation at a Bowery flophouse!"

"What a tongue-lashing!" He smirked. "I know just the revenge I'd like to take." The tone of his voice had become even more suggestive than his words.

"Let's talk about the weather," she retorted dryly.

"I finished talking about that. You weren't listening. You were too busy figuring out why I wouldn't make a good leader." He laughed.

"Somebody should have told you by now that tact is essential for a good leader," she sniffed.

"I thought you had finished your lecture." He shook his head. "How wrong can a guy be? Sounds like you know a lot about leading. Tell you what I'll do. Seeing as you know the number-one trait, tact, I'll give you the lead up Black Dike."

Dumbfounded, Dana stared at him. Like a mindless fish, she was caught again, and by the same hook. She knew and she knew that he knew there was no way she could lead up a six-hundred-foot icicle.

"If I lead, how will you know I can follow?" she stammered.

Though his mouth was drawn in a tight line, his eyes seemed to be laughing. "I'll take it on faith." He stuck his thumbs in his belt while he watched her.

Unable to contain her frustration, Dana stamped her heel against the rich nub of the wool carpeting. "Do you enjoy seeing me squirm?" she asked petulantly.

"Yes."

"Well, I don't enjoy squirming. And I don't think you have any intention of letting me lead. You just . . . you just have sadistic tendencies!"

"You bring them out in me," he said. "I don't know why. Maybe it's your calm reserve that I want to shake up. Women like you ought to be illegal. You have everything —beauty, wealth, courage, talent. You're the kind of woman who's immortalized in celluloid, the kind who glitters and dazzles. Yet there's something else. I can't get a fix on you."

"You should have asked me to send in an autobiography along with my application. But if you want to know the truth, I can't get a fix on you either. However, since we're only contemplating a couple of climbs together and not a marriage, that doesn't really matter. As long as you know I'm not a madwoman who intends to cut your rope while you're dangling hundreds of feet over jagged rock, and as long as I know you're not going to lead me into a bottomless abyss or leave me somewhere with a broken leg as carrion for the vultures, we should be okay."

"You don't mess around, do you?" he asked rhetorically. "I like that. You don't put on airs or pretend to be what you're not."

Dana flushed, all too aware of the role she was playing. "Even if what I'm not is what I should be?" she asked mockingly.

"Wait a minute. You're confusing me."

"Don't you think I ought to be walking barefoot among the peasants somewhere? Don't you think it's disgusting to come from Scarsdale and wear lavender sweat suits, especially when you're not sweating?"

"Disgusting is a strong word," he said.

48

"You're right. Let's substitute outrageous, repulsive, abhorrent, offensive. Take your pick."

"That's not the way I would choose to live," he said evenly.

"I'm glad. A lavender sweat suit wouldn't look good on you. Meanwhile," she hesitated, "you were kidding about letting me lead, weren't you?"

"Yes."

"What a sense of humor! When you get tired of climbing, maybe Johnny Carson will let you cohost the *Tonight* show." Dana stopped talking suddenly. To her own ears her voice sounded high-pitched and nervous. She had been talking up a storm, she realized, and if asked to repeat what she had said she would have been at a loss.

Gary didn't respond to her attempt at lightness. "I'll be right back," he said as he walked out the front door.

Undoubtedly the man is fed up with this game we've been playing, she thought.

He was back in a few minutes, carrying a thick rope. "What do you think of this? It's a full eleven millimeters thick. You know, of course, that we'll have to double our belay anchors and use two ice pitons or screws."

Dana handled the rope that would be used for belaying. It was only recently that she had learned the origins of belaying. It was first discovered by sailors who learned that a rope wound around a post allowed a man to pull in a fish that would normally pull him twenty feet into the air. Mountaineers have modified the technique by using their own bodies as the post and by anchoring themselves to the rock. The friction on the rope absorbs so much weight that the climber can support another person who is dangling in the air as easily as he could support a puppy.

"It's a sturdy rope," Dana said. "It will be able to

handle the heavy loading. Do you think hard hats will be necessary?"

"Probably not, but we can use them anyway. Well," he said with a note of finality in his voice, "I guess we've covered the equipment. Do you want to meet me at the ski lodge in two weeks, Wednesday, say about three in the morning?"

"Three A.M. it is." Dana knew he wanted to complete the climb before the noon sun might have a chance to melt some of the ice or snow.

Gary was gathering up the equipment that lay on the floor. "One thing before I go," he said with a serious, almost remote expression in his eyes, "don't let me bully you into anything you're not comfortable doing. If you're not absolutely sure about climbing the Black Dike, I don't want you to do it. It would be no cause for shame. Remember, there's never just one expedition. There's always another one. And there's always a better climber. It's got to come from within."

"I know what I want," she answered.

Just as she was walking over to the front door with Gary, an easy smile on her face, the buzzer sounded. Flinging the portal wide, her heart sank.

"The gold braid is missing on this one too," Gary kidded.

A real messenger this time stood laden with boxes in front of her.

"Miss Manchester? Will you sign for these, please?"

"Here's where I came in," Gary spoke up.

She thought she saw amusement, or was it exasperation, in his smile.

"I liked that blue dress you were wearing, myself. But you never know when you'll find something better." He started down the driveway, stopping at the pile of boxes that stood on the sidewalk next to the van that had BOUTIQUE ELEGANTE painted on its side. "Hey!" he shouted. "Are you sure you're D. Manchester, the mountain climber?"

"No," she shouted back. "I'm D. Manchester, the social climber. The mountain climber is in the back room trying on combat boots!"

Dana spent the remainder of the day trying on clothes, an exhausting exercise. Thoughts of Gary intruded. He was strange. It seemed to her that like an iceberg, most of what was Gary LeBlanc remained hidden beneath the surface. What did he think of her? Did he like her? Did he disapprove as much as he appeared to? And why should she care? And why was she pretending to be someone she was not? In truth she probably had even less interest in material riches than he. For the first time in years Dana baffled herself.

Just before she fell into a fitful sleep late that night, her eyes fastened on the one and only needlepoint she had ever done, framed and hung across from her bed. It was a saying by e. e. cummings.

TO BE NOBODY BUT YOURSELF IN A WORLD WHICH IS DOING ITS BEST, NIGHT AND DAY, TO MAKE YOU EVERYBODY ELSE MEANS TO FIGHT THE HARDEST BATTLE ANY HUMAN BEING CAN FIGHT AND NEVER STOP FIGHTING.

CHAPTER THREE

The black night was pure and still. A cold moon hung overhead, illuminating the snow and ice that lay everywhere. A frozen spot of fear which she could not acknowledge lay in her heart. The only sounds were of her chill breath and of the hammering, the testing, the hammering again from ten feet above. She ignored the crick that was starting in her neck, for she could not take her eyes from the burnished face and the powerful form above her. She knew she was handing her life over to Gary and she watched with a certain fear and a certain pride as he moved slowly up the icicle in smooth advances and pauses, changing positions, testing holds, flexing fingers in an endless succession of repetitious acts.

It was this beginning of a climb that was always the worst for Dana. Before she felt her body responding and molding to the rock or the snow she was afraid, for she was too aware of the hidden dangers that awaited her, to be revealed when least expected. Ice climbing was not like scaling rock, which had a constancy to it. Ice changed with the weather, with the time of day, with the calendar. This waiting for a signal from Gary, with the silence of ice all around her, with the blackness swirling in the wind, was a test of her toughness.

"Off belay." His voice cut through the stillness of the night.

She started climbing, unsure at first, slipping, sliding, before she began to feel a familiarity with her movements. Right from the start the climb was steep so that she had to kick her crampons with all her might. The two spikes that point straight ahead ground into the ice, allowing her to put full weight on them. Like many women climbers, Dana lacked great strength in her arms, for which she had to compensate with the adroit use of feet and legs.

The sound of her crampons was brittle. She worked efficiently, absorbed in the rhythm of her climb. Thoughts of falling down the glassy incline gradually left her as a secret happiness filled her. She was alone with Gary on this planet, the two mighty conquerors. Her mind emptied of daily cares, and if someone had spoken to her of Halston or Dior, she would not have recognized the names. Her mind and body became one efficient machine, and though the climb was harder than she had thought possible, with few holds in the slick, ungiving ice, she felt triumphant. With Gary above her, chopping, judging, testing, sometimes spread-eagled against the ice as if he were supporting it she knew she was safe. Her faith in him became blind and absolute. Her concentration on him and on each hold that he found or forged became complete. The giant icicle that they were tackling became a living, palpable monster which they had set out to tame. She lost track of time as little by little they climbed higher and higher. Her hands became numbed with the cold and she had to flex her fingers constantly to avoid losing sensation in them. A slick glaze of ice covered the rope, making it slippery and hard to grasp. The icicle was unyielding, refusing to give the smallest hold, forcing each step to be labored and time-consuming.

"See that overhang? It's got a nice ledge underneath." Gary pointed four yards to the left of him. "Come on up."

"Climbing," she acknowledged as she signaled him to take up the slack in the rope.

She moved rapidly over the area that Gary had so painstakingly charted. Knowing he was watching her from his perch, she moved with an added grace, feeling as if she could fly. Where one step was not enough to keep her balance she would follow it in quick succession with a second and a third. Her steps appeared choreographed, almost as if she were a prima ballerina. Each of her movements was sure and deliberate. She had never climbed better.

When she reached him, Gary was pouring her fruit punch from his canteen. Gratefully she drained the mug of the metallic-tasting liquid. She watched as he tore off a large heel of French bread and a hunk of cheese. He served himself in the same manner and sat down next to her on the glassy seat in which he had driven pitons with which to attach the rope and themselves. In between bites Dana rubbed her hands together, trying to increase circulation.

"Let me help you with that," he said as he lifted her hands to blow on them with hot breath. "Long, slender fingers—you have good climbing hands."

As though his breath were that of a fire-breathing dragon she pulled back.

"I—I," she stammered. "Could I have more punch?"

Silent, he obliged.

"I understand now why you're considered such a phenomenon," she said to cover the nervousness that had overcome her. "A climb like this would take most people twenty minutes per foot. You must be breaking speed records."

"It's just experience," he answered modestly. "After a while you know where to hit with your hammer, where the ice will give. I brought along a special dessert. Do you like yogurt-covered peanuts?"

"I never tried them," she answered with a smile.

"Close your eyes and open your mouth," he ordered playfully.

Unthinkingly, she obeyed. In a flash she realized it was his kiss that she was hoping for rather than his candy.

It was his candy that she got.

"Delicious," she pronounced, as she imagined the sugar pumping up her veins with instant energy. "Fifty more of these and I'll be ready to attain the summit in one sweep."

He smiled at her and lapsed into silence. Together they looked out over a panorama of white hills and a starry sky that was beginning to lighten. For a split-second fantasy she thought that she felt closer to Gary than she had ever felt to another human being. He knew about a mountain's majesty and he knew the primitive thrill of doing what other people only dreamed about.

"This high above ordinary mortals, and yogurt-covered peanuts begin to taste like manna from the ancient Greek gods," he said fancifully.

"We are the last of the great romantics, aren't we?" she asked with the same whimsy.

"Maybe. We are among those who seek the unreachable. Could be we're nuts." He laughed.

Dana looked at him soberly. "I'm a nut. At least everybody else seems to think I am, but I don't think you are."

It was a strange look that Gary cast upon her, a look that made the tiny hairs on the back of her neck stand on end.

"We ought to get going," he said after a lapse of several minutes.

They cleaned up the remains of their repast and Dana secured her stance as she watched him deftly scale the slippery face of the Black Dike.

The sun was rising and her muscles were cramped and cold from sitting. Her hands fumbled as she sought the handkerchief in her pocket to wipe her frozen nose. Suddenly there was a roar in the sky and the whirring of a helicopter just above them.

"Son of a . . . !" Gary cried out. "It's a weather 'copter, reporting ski conditions of the slope."

Dana half pirouetted on the ledge that held her, failing to observe and consider the movement. A sharp pain pierced her calf, followed by a sticky, warm sensation. Looking around wildly, she saw the point of a small icicle sticking ominously into her leg. Groaning, she moved gingerly away from the frozen needle. She searched in her pocket for her large white handkerchief. Bending painfully, she reached up through her pants to dab at the gash. The handkerchief came out soaked with blood. She bit her lip in vexation. It wasn't that bad an injury, and after a minute she knew the pain would cease. However, she feared a stiffening in her limb. Bending again, she tied the handkerchief around her calf.

"Give me ten minutes, Gary," she called out. The bleeding would surely stop by them.

"Sure. Anything the matter?" he asked.

"No, I just feel like a rest. Would you say we're about midway?"

"Not quite. Still, we ought to make the summit in good time. You want something to drink?"

"Sure," she answered.

He lowered a canteen to her by rope. Grasping it, she took a long gulp of sweet liquid. Her leg was throbbing now, her mind confused. Common sense dictated that she tell Gary what had happened. Stubbornness wouldn't let her. She had to finish this climb. She had to. The accident was her fault. She had allowed herself to become unhinged by the unexpected noise of the helicopter. A climber had to maintain his or her wits at all times. Nothing must be permitted to interfere with concentration and caution. The smallest mistake could mean a fatality. Each movement, each gesture, had to be planned. Nothing could be casual. She hadn't thought out that silly turn she had made. A mistake like that could have been her last.

For the uninitiated, climbing was a risky sport. To people like Gary and Dana it was hard, exhilarating, and still risky. They liked to think, however, that the risk for them was minimal. Because they planned what they did, there was always a back-up. If a foothold broke, there should be a handhold. If that proved ineffective, there was the rope. And if the rope should snap or slip, there were methods of self-arrest in mid-fall. Events were prepared for. And now this! Dana thought miserably. What had possessed her to be so careless? She calculated that if she could last a few more hours on the leg, there was a chance she might get off scot-free. Maybe she would be lucky and this wound would be one of those that showed their effects the next day. She had to give it a try.

"On belay," she called up to Gary as she finished retying the rope around her.

She felt the rope tauten and she recommenced her climb. The joy that had filled her heart was gone. She had made an error and it was through sheer luck that she had suffered only a cut leg.

Putting herself on automatic pilot, she heaved and hoisted, stepping quickly when it was called for, waiting when Gary had trouble finding a fissure for an ice screw. The throbbing in her leg was getting worse, and she was losing elasticity. This wasn't fair to Gary, she decided.

Stopping, she took a deep breath and yelled, "Off belay." She lifted her leg slowly. "Gary, I have to tell you something." She swallowed the lump that was threatening to rise in her throat.

"Something the matter?" he called down.

"Yes. Something is the matter." She heard her voice crack.

"You tired? We can rest a little more if you like." He was concerned. There was nothing judgmental in his tone.

"No, I'm not tired. I got hurt, Gary. It's nothing serious, but, well, I thought I ought to tell you."

"How bad?"

"It's just a little scrape on my leg. Nothing really." She was regretting her decision to tell him. She should have been more stoical.

"Let me see." He had climbed quickly down to stand beside her.

"It's not worth the trouble." She laughed giddily. "I just figured I'd better tell the scout leader. Scouting rules you know."

"Let me see."

Pressing her lips so tightly together that they became one thin line, Dana rolled up her pant leg. The white handkerchief had turned red. As she untied it she thought she was going to be sick. The puncture wound was deep, raw, and ragged. It had bled profusely, more so than she had been aware.

Gently, Gary examined the leg, cleaning it with antiseptic and bandaging it with gauze. "We'll make our descent," he said decisively.

Though the descent was often trickier and more difficult than the ascent, it was faster. Gary had left the pitons and ice screws in place so that all testing and searching was cut out. All he had to do was to clip a carabiner around the piton and slip the rope through it. They would be down quickly. Her feet were light, for she forced herself to forget the pain. Her heart was heavy. To have come this far, to actually be halfway up the Black Dike with one of the world's great climbers leading and then to have it all come crashing down on her head, that was too much to bear. She had been so happy on the way up. She had felt as if she belonged here with Gary. She had been at peace. She had been herself.

"How's the leg holding up?" he yelled. The wind carried away his voice, but Dana had been staring so intently at his mouth when he stopped to look up at her that she had managed to lipread his question.

"Not too bad," she called back into the whistling wind.

He gestured with one arm out as if presenting her with a gift. The golden edge of the sun was rising over the peaks and slopes of the White Mountains.

"So beautiful," she said.

She read his lips again. "Like you." Perhaps she had

imagined him mouthing those words, she thought as she followed him, slowly, painfully.

Her leg propped up in front of a roaring fire, Dana sipped a cup of steaming coffee. Gary sat across from her, hunched forward, his coffee between his hands. The fire leaped and flickered, red and blue, orange and green.

"I don't know why they're using an artificial log," Gary muttered, disgruntled.

Dana didn't answer. She stared out the picture window with her chin jutting out from under her pouting lips. Early morning skiers were straggling off the T-bar determined that their tracks should be the first on the virgin snow.

A feeling of gloom crushed Dana. Each time Gary started to speak, the foreboding that he was about to utter the words she knew were coming made her feel as though she couldn't breathe. How could she entertain the smallest hope that he was still considering her for McKinley? She had aborted a mere six-hundred-foot climb not even midway. She had been careless. No responsible leader could take a chance on someone like her again.

The sounds of laughter floated in through the open door. How carefree those skiers seemed. She just hoped that when he gave her the ax he would do it kindly. Just don't let him tell her to go back to Scarsdale for some tennis!

"How are you feeling?" His voice broke into her thoughts.

"I dunno," she answered in a monotone.

"We ought to let a doctor look at that. You might need a stitch or two."

"I'll be all right," she answered shortly. Why did he

have to prolong the agony with kindness? she wondered. "Sorry I ruined your climb."

"You didn't ruin anything," he answered. "Accidents happen. It was understandable with that ridiculous helicopter."

"Sure," she said.

Lifting her head back, she drained the coffee cup. As she lowered the cup to the table at her side she kept her head back. If she concentrated on something else, like the random black marks on the ceiling, maybe the pain that she knew was in her eyes would disappear before he could see it. There was no sense in making this harder for either of them than it had to be.

"Let's go. I want you to get that leg taken care of," he reiterated.

"Don't worry about it."

"If you're going to go trekking across the glacier on Karstens Ridge, you've got to be in tiptop shape." He held out his hand to pull her up.

Too taken by his words to notice the proferred hand, Dana sat bolt upright. She searched his face. "Are you, to coin a bad pun, pulling my leg?"

"I wouldn't do a thing like that." He laughed.

"I don't understand. I failed the test. I blew it. Mission not accomplished."

Gary's voice took on a grave expression. "Success can't be measured in only one way. You're an excellent climber. That was easy enough to see. What's also apparent is your common sense. I believe you could have finished the climb even with your leg cut up like that. And I believe that you knew it. But you chose the honorable way. You told me. And that took courage, more courage than you would have needed to continue to the top, even with that throbbing you were feeling. You and I both know that what is a minor inconvenience on the ground gets all pumped up on a climb like this. So you wouldn't have only been taking a chance with your life, but with mine, not to mention with the success of the climb. I never wanted a hot dog on my team. I want the members of my team to know they're part of a team. Telling me about your leg was right. You let me be the judge."

"Not bad for a fancy lady from Scarsdale, huh?" she teased, overcoming a powerful desire to throw her arms around his neck and thank him from the bottom of her heart.

"I wouldn't want to live there," he answered in kind, "but I've got to give Scarsdale credit for growing at least one tough, smart lady."

He reached out his hand to stroke her cheek, his fingers warm and smooth like a stone eroded by wind and water. When he withdrew his hand she felt it still, as if the memory were imprinted in her pores. When their eyes met it was as if an elemental flash of recognition passed between them. She felt it as a fluttering deep inside her and she felt it as a heavy-heartedness replacing her elation. Had he meant what he said? Did he know she was good, or was it his desire for her that was skewing his judgment? If she looked like a roller derby queen, would he still, after today's fiasco, want her to climb Mount McKinley with him?

"Gary, are you sure?"

"My team doesn't question my decisions." His eyebrows were knit as he studied her. "Are you sure you want to come along? Have you considered the rigors of this climb? It won't be like climbing the Rockies or even Rainier. We're liable to run into some brutal conditions. And there will be no blazing fireplace and soft chair in the event of an ice splinter or a change of heart. It won't be what you're used to."

"What I'm used to is what I've been running away from my whole life," she said.

"You are sure this is what you want? Perhaps you ought to work it out on an analyst's couch rather than on a climb."

Her eyes blazed. "I have nothing more to work out than you do. Probably a lot less. I don't carry a lot of prejudicial baggage around with me.

"Prejudiced? Who me?"

"Yes, you. If all my clothes came from a bargain basement and my hair was a stringy, greasy mess, I'd have a lot less to prove." She stopped in mid-thought. Why this harangue? Hadn't she just gotten what she wanted? Her voice became less strident, softer. "I'd be honored to be a member of your team."

"Glad to have you," he said. "Let's celebrate with some pastry."

"You don't seem like the pastry type," Dana observed.

"You mean I'm not flaky?" Gary laughed. "Well, whenever I finish a climb, even a short one, I have some pastry. I smell hot, gooey cinnamon buns. Do you want one?"

"There's nothing I'd like better," Dana said, suddenly aware of hunger pangs. She gazed at him as he walked toward the snack bar and thought that he had the same easy gait and self-assured manner whether at the Oak Room in New York, at her parents' home in Scarsdale, or here at the lodge. Whatever faults he might have, Dana thought he was straight and honest.

Returning, Gary informed Dana, "There was only one

left. We'll have to share." Breaking the large sweet roll into halves, he offered her a piece. "Careful, it's sticky." His hand and the warm caramel topping touched her palm and a strange combination of hungers passed through her. "Getting back to your statement—if your clothes came from a bargain basement and your hair was a stringy, greasy mess, yes, you still would have made the team."

"Really?" Dana questioned happily.

"Yes, but I wouldn't have shared my cinnamon roll with you!"

Smiling, they walked out to the rented car which Gary had parked in the lodge's lot.

"You'll want to meet the other members. They're both New Englanders. So Boston seems a reasonable place to get together. How about in a couple of weeks? Your place?"

"Fine. I'll be spending the intervening time getting things together."

"When you pack make sure you leave out your comb."

"You couldn't resist that, could you?" she smiled.

The drive back to Boston was uneventful. The conversation remained light, the tone neutral. During the long silences that sometimes occurred, Dana mulled over the events of the day. It was true that she had climbed well, but it was also true that the "accident" was no accident. It was the result of her carelessness. Gary had deliberately chosen to overlook that and it puzzled her. It also puzzled her that her eyes remained riveted on the large hands that held the steering wheel, sometimes moving to the arms bulging with muscles and veins. He had removed his jacket in the car and rolled up his sleeves so that the sun glinted off the black hair that lightly covered his forearms.

Gary's dark eyes, even when he spoke to her, remained fixed on the road ahead.

As they entered Boston proper, Gary asked if he could drop her off at an emergency room somewhere.

"No. If you insist though, I'll see a doctor. There's a nice, doddering physician on my corner whose expertise is more than sufficient for what ails me."

"Just make sure he doesn't leave any scars on that gorgeous limb."

"You're a flatterer."

"No. Do you want me to go with you?"

"To the doctor?" Dana laughed. "To hold my hand? I'm a big girl."

"I'll wait for you in the car then."

"What for?" she asked.

"To drive you home."

"It's on the same block," she reminded him.

"Maybe you'll take pity on a tired mountaineer and invite him in for a drink and . . ."

"And?"

"And peanuts." He laughed more heartily than necessary.

"I'm out of peanuts and I'm out of drinks. I'm also out of hospitality. Do you really want me on your team?" She said it all in one breath, without waiting for a break, as if it were one thought.

"Are you afraid there are strings attached?" he asked coldly.

"I'm afraid there's a sixteen-millimeter rope attached," she answered.

"I don't play that way," he assured her. "Sure, I'd like you in my bed. I'd also like you on my team. One is not

65

·dependent on the other. I thought we'd been through this already." He frowned.

"I'm a slow learner."

"Slow is one thing you could never be accused of. There are other things, though, that I could say about you," he offered.

"Don't." Though she kept her tone light, Dana was dead serious, since she could imagine what those other things were, and she was in no mood to hear them. Be happy! she told herself. You're going. You got what you wanted! Yet doubts about Gary's motivation nagged at her. He knew she had made an error in judgment on the Dike, that she had let her concentration lapse. Yet he dismissed the evidence, saying that accidents happen. Maybe his answer was valid. But, she argued, what did it matter? She was going. That was the crucial issue. If he had told her she was out of the running, she would have been miserable and would have cursed him as a chauvinist. Here she had heard what she most wanted to hear and she cursed him as an opportunist. It was a classic double bind that she had designed. He was damned if he did and damned if he didn't. Maybe this was simply a manufactured problem. Maybe she was creating a problem where none existed, she thought morosely.

The silence in the car was becoming oppressive. Apparently Gary thought so, too, for he started a couple of conversational gambits, both of which led nowhere. "So how do you like living in Boston?" he asked.

"It's all right." Dead end. Be sociable! Dana told herself furiously. "It's convenient for climbing," she added.

After another few minutes of silence Gary said, "You'd better direct me," nosing the car through the winding streets.

"The doctor's office is in that little red building," she said as he entered the street where she lived. "I can just walk in without an appointment."

Her leg, when she stepped out of the car onto the curb, pained her so that she could barely put pressure on it. She amended her statement. "I should have said, I can limp in without an appointment."

Thin-lipped, Gary parked the car and walked around to the passenger side. "Lean on me and keep quiet."

"Gary," she laughed. "You're acting as if I'm one of the war wounded. I was kidding about having to limp." She noticed him flush. "I appreciate your chivalry, it's sweet, but not necessary."

The flush disappeared to be replaced by a stern look. Gary bent and effortlessly scooped her up in his arms and carried her to the doctor's doorstep. Impressed by his strength but annoyed at the treatment, Dana decided to say nothing.

Letting her down gently at the door, Gary said, "There are no strings attached. You're quite a capable, sensible climber. Whatever more you are is irrelevant." He kissed her hard and returned to his car, leaving her standing there, dazed and balancing on one foot.

CHAPTER FOUR

To Dana, Boston was an exciting place to live. The only problem was that it didn't feel like home. But then again, no place felt like home. As a professional mountaineer Dana had long been an itinerant. The only constant for her was the mountains. For a while she had lived in Washington state near the foot of Mount Rainier. Having been selected from among numerous candidates to work for the Rainier Mountaineering Guide Service, the most prestigious guide group in the country, she had been only too happy to move from one coast to the other. But within a month she had been called back east on "urgent" family business and had not returned. The job she had during the warm weather, guiding in the White Mountains of New Hampshire, suited her for the time being, even though it was only a summer job. Only the hardiest of folk chose to climb in the winter. For Dana, however, climbing was a year-round pleasure which she indulged in for two or three-day excursions. Whether it was inertia or simply that she enjoyed Boston, which kept her in the northeast this winter, she wasn't certain. The office temp work she had been doing on and off was fun sometimes, but not something she wanted to commit herself to.

Walking in Harvard Square, Dana was utterly absorbed in the street scenes. The men, intense, bearded, preppy, or crew-necked, the women, peasanty or chic, all seemed terribly intelligent. Perhaps, like her, they were just passersby and only their proximity to the venerated ivy halls of Harvard University lent them, in her mind, personas that mirrored enormous I.Q.'s. In any case, Dana enjoyed people-watching, particularly in Cambridge.

Apparently others enjoyed people-watching, too, or, at least, the men enjoyed Dana-watching, for she couldn't help but notice that she garnered her fair share of interested glances. That, however, was something Dana was used to.

Cambridge, besides being full of interesting people, was full of interesting shops. It was easy for Dana to while away hours browsing among the curios. Passing a candlemaker, she could not resist the purchase of a pair of hand-dipped yellow and orange candles, which, although they would clash dreadfully with her furnishings, were too pretty to resist. Next she found herself in a shop overflowing with antique clothing. No one, she knew, would ever think Dana a collector of old clothes. She loved the quiet elegance of the turn of the century costumes which had little in common with current fashion. This time she found a silk shawl made in Poland one hundred years ago. It was decorated with delicate hand-embroidered flowers in vivid colors which had not faded with the years.

As she left the store, the proud owner of the shawl, she marveled that for the first time in weeks the focus of her thoughts had not been on Gary. But now her mind raced with Gary-related thoughts, for the meeting he had set up with the other two climbers was in just two days. There was still so much she had to do. First and foremost was buying the food and drink. There was a beer and soft drink outlet that she passed on her way home. That was one thing, at least, that she could accomplish today.

The store was crowded, the checkout boy new, and as Dana waited on the supermarketlike line, she shifted her weight from one foot to the other. It was then that she noticed the man in the line next to hers. His wavy black hair hung over his eyes, a cigarette dangled from the corner of his mouth, and his eyes bored into her. The steadiness of his gaze unnerved her. She turned her back to him, but could somehow still feel his eyes. It was with relief that she finally paid for her purchases and pushed her cart to her car.

As she was slamming her trunk shut, a surprisingly gentle voice sounded behind her. The black-haired man was asking if she cared to share an alfalfa sprout salad and bean curd at the vegetarian restaurant on the corner.

"No, thanks," she said automatically, jumping back slightly.

"You are a vegetarian, aren't you?" the man persisted. "You don't look like a carnivore."

"I eat only Big Macs," she said, smiling, refusing further conversation.

As quietly as he had come, the man retreated.

Driving away, Dana was relieved. That encounter had proven surprisingly easy to handle. And that assessment, she noted a couple of red lights later, had been erroneous.

There he was again, pulling up beside her in a beat-up foreign car, his face pulled into a lecherous leer.

"Can I drink your bath water?" he was asking through his open window.

"Pervert!" she shouted as she pressed hard on the accelerator, making her vehicle spurt ahead.

Oh, for the purity of the mountains and fellow mountaineers! She felt a pressing urge to get away from the city with its "interesting" inhabitants.

It wasn't as if Dana had never been approached by a weirdo before. Goodness knows, all sorts of men in every conceivable circumstance approached her. It was just that she yearned for the challenge of a peak that she had not yet climbed. She yearned to be judged for what she could do and not for the way she looked. Sometimes she even wished she had been born plain. Plain women knew that if they were sought after, it was for who they really were. And Dana could so easily do without the ubiquitous male advances. It was, she thought wryly, a lot easier to divest herself from the trappings of wealth than from the trappings of beauty.

Yawning, Dana opened one eye. And closed it again. Tuesday. It was finally here. This was the day for which she had planned, read up on Alaska, done fifty push-ups daily, shopped, stocked up on beer, encountered that silly pervert, cleaned her closets for no earthly reason she could comprehend, and dreaded. She pulled the covers over her head. It was seven o'clock. She had five hours until Gary came with Bill Lewis and Joe Flynn. Five hours to fret. Neither she nor Gary had mentioned lunch, but the meeting was set for twelve noon. Not wanting to appear as if she were hostessing a Scarsdale luncheon, Dana had decided on a simple buffet of cold meats and salads, rolls and cheeses. That ought to cover all bases.

She tried to fall asleep again. If she could sleep longer, she would have less time to worry about the meeting. Dealing with Gary was bad enough, but he had assured her that the other team members would hate her. There was nothing like encouragement, she thought wryly. She wondered if he had told them about her "accident." If so, they were sure to have more to say about it than he had. Well, if they were going to be gunning for her, she ought to have an artillery of her own. She did. She had boned up on every new piece of equipment on the market. She had studied weather maps and charts of Mount McKinley. She had read all published accounts of previous climbs or attempts made upon it. She could talk about the charlatans who had claimed to reach its summit as well as about the unprepared barroom adventurers, the sourdoughs, who, in less than one day with no more provisions than as if they were going out for a picnic, had come within three hundred feet of its summit. She had memorized all pertinent facts and she could reel them off, she thought amusedly, until her guests dropped from boredom. If only her facts, figures, corned beef, pickles, and nice smile would be enough to thwart the animosity she anticipated.

Dragging herself out of bed, she stumbled into the shower. The water, which due to faulty plumbing alternated between scalding and freezing, woke her up. She brushed her hair, put on a touch of mascara, pulled on, for no reason she could fathom other than perversity, her lavender sweat suit, and thought again about the upcoming meeting.

After a breakfast of dry cereal and juice, she glanced around her studio apartment. A refugee from her mother's knick-knack mania, her own living quarters were decorated to the point of starkness. The only personal touches were the plants in plain clay pots scattered throughout the room. Her furniture was bland though of good quality. A brown and white herringbone sofa and two molded wooden chairs from Denmark dominated the available space. From her closet she took out two folding director's chairs with the insignia of the local educational television station emblazoned on the canvas. The remainder of the closet was jammed with the gifts her parents sent at every opportunity. Her mother's greatest pleasure was shopping. She loved to give. Dana hated to receive. As a result, the Limoges china from last Christmas was still unwrapped, the silver tureen for New Year's stood tarnished in its box. The Lladro figurines of a veterinarian, a tennis player, and a pianist, which she had gotten for Arbor Day, Presidents' Day, and Valentine's Day gathered dust, and her last birthday present, a hand-painted porcelain music box which played Liberace sat on the floor in the darkest corner of the closet.

Something, one of her demons Dana thought later, made her pause as she started to close the closet door. Standing on tiptoe, she reached up to fill her arms with the gray figurines. Her mother, she thought amusedly, was the type of person who would travel to Spain, not to gaze in awe at Granada or to shout her olés at the bullfight, but to fill empty suitcases with Lladro straight from the factory. She surveyed her room once more. And then she placed the figurines wherever they would be most prominent. Next she took down the carton of Limoges china. She had bought paper plates, but now was as good a time as any to christen the new dishes. After all, she thought sardonically, she wouldn't want to disappoint Gary by not living up to his expectations.

By the time noon rolled around Dana had successfully changed the face of her apartment. All hints of asceticism had been adroitly covered up so that now it resembled a *House Beautiful* ad. The doorbell rang as she was folding the last linen napkin.

"Hello. Come on in." A wide smile was fixed on her face.

As the two men who stood behind Gary trooped past her they introduced themselves. They were as different in appearance from each other and from Gary as could be imagined. Whereas Gary was tall, lean, and dangerously handsome, Bill Lewis looked as if he had arrived on the same spaceship as E.T. He was short, skinny, with an oversize, egg-shaped cranium, a wide forehead, receding hairline, and horn-rimmed glasses. He was, he told Dana, a software engineer and a genius. He was not, Dana thought, humble. Joe Flynn was squat, broad, with heavy dark eyebrows, a full jaw, and a bulbous nose. He was a high school science teacher on sabbatical.

"And what do *you* do?" Bill Lewis asked as he stretched himself out on the floor.

"A little of this, a little of that," Dana answered, sitting up straight in a corner of her sofa. "My commitment is to climbing."

"I see," said Bill Lewis.

He didn't see at all, Dana thought. Or maybe he saw too much. She noticed the corners of Gary's lips twitching as though it were an effort to keep a straight face.

"Please, help yourself," she indicated the laden table.

Bill Lewis and Gary made their sandwiches and poured

their drinks. An unintelligible sound, something like *arghnmph* came from Joe Flynn's direction.

"I beg your pardon?" Dana said quickly.

"Be—ahh," Joe repeated more clearly.

"If you'd like a beer, Joe, they're right over there," she pointed to the part of the table nearest to him.

From the corner of her eye she spied Gary smiling amusedly.

"I have a tentative list of expenses, everyone," Gary said. "A big one is going to be the snow plane we charter to take us to the Muldrow Glacier and to pick us up. Supplies, equipment, emergency back-up," he read from a list. "You're going to be laying out a tidy sum, somewhere in the neighborhood of twelve thousand each. Anybody have a problem with that?"

No one spoke.

After a bit Bill propped himself up on one elbow and drawled, "The three of us men have careers. Should your estimate fall low, we'll be able to raise extra funds. But this young lady here. Does she have the wherewithal to pull her weight? And I guess I mean that in more ways than one."

"Why don't you ask her yourself?" Gary said smoothly. "Besides, knowing how to climb she knows how to talk."

"Money won't be a problem for me," Dana put in quickly.

"How convenient," Bill Lewis sniffed, sensing inherited wealth, to him a sign of absolute moral turpitude. "How long you been climbing?"

"Five years. How long have . . . you been climbing?" she answered with a question of her own.

"Long enough. You belong to a climbing club in college or something like that?"

"As a matter of fact I didn't climb at all in college. Not even the steps." She hoped her feeble attempt at a joke would lighten the tone of what was turning into an inquisition.

"Gary says you're good," Bill Lewis said not so much as a compliment but as a challenge.

In an attempt to turn the tables, Dana nodded as if that was understood. "I hear you're good too. I understand you've climbed in the Andes and the Alps."

Bill shrugged one shoulder dismissively as if to say, Dana thought, that such trivial accomplishments as having climbed some of the world's most forbidding mountains were not worth his discussing.

Joe Flynn slathered mustard on his third club sandwich. He reached for his fourth beer, then belched.

As uninvolved as if he were watching a movie, Gary sat back on the couch, one leg folded over the other. He took a long sip of his Coke.

"You ski?" Lewis asked.

"Enough for our purposes," Dana answered crisply. "I assume we're going to be using skis for transportation of supplies on the glacier?"

"That's right," Gary rejoined approvingly.

"Good," Dana said. "Besides saving us time, skis will also lessen the danger of falling through snow-hidden crevasses."

Bill Lewis didn't say anything, though she saw a flicker of respect in his eyes. He reached for a cream-cheese-filled celery stalk.

"You had much experience with cold weather?" Bill Lewis continued his interrogation.

"She *is* cold weather," Gary joked.

Joe Flynn guffawed, the first human sound he had uttered since his arrival.

Dana pursed her lips. She was becoming progressively more annoyed. "If Gary is satisfied with my experience, the matter should be closed."

Joe Flynn winked broadly at Gary. "Ya satisfied, LeBlanc?"

So, Dana thought wickedly, the man did know how to talk.

"Dana acquitted herself very well on the Black Dike," Gary stated.

Acquitted, that was a good choice of word, Dana thought. She was, after all was said and done, on trial. And why should it be she rather than big-headed Bill Lewis or simian-faced Joe Flynn who had to be questioned so rudely. Indeed, she had never heard of them before. She had to take their credentials on faith, on Gary's say-so, just as they had to accept hers.

"She's coming with us men," Gary continued. There was a steel-edged note to his voice. "Get used to it. You've got only one other choice." He didn't elaborate.

Flynn, his mouth full, stopped chewing. Lewis's face went a shade whiter. Dana felt warmed, as though she had swallowed a full shot glass of cognac.

"I want to be prepared to start out the second week in April. All supplies should be laid in by then and our course thoroughly charted. It will be too early for any significant melting and temperatures should be up by then to maybe ten or fifteen below, if we're lucky."

"Maybe we should reconsider and climb a volcano in Hawaii," Dana joked, knowing full well that nobody climbed volcanos. As irritated as she had been by Lewis and Flynn, she felt a bit sorry for them. They looked like tomcats who had been booted in the gut by their owner. And they were, after all, guests in her home.

"Joe, I have a dessert that you're going to love. And I bet you'll like it too, Bill. It's a lemon meringue mousse I whipped up last night."

Whipped up, was a slight understatement, she thought amusedly. In a flight of fancy she had gotten out her one and only and rarely opened cookbook. Maybe it was out of guilt, she had ruminated, for the delicatessen luncheon she was serving. In any case, putting all her creative effort into it, and with an open picture of Mount McKinley by her side, she had labored all evening over the mousse, finally succeeding in fashioning it into a facsimile of the peak they were aiming to conquer. On the very top she had stuck a toothpick with a little paper American flag.

"Way to go!" Joe Flynn cheered as she entered. He became suddenly garrulous. "If that tastes as good as it looks, nothing's going to stop you from comin' along. Imagine what she could do with a can of baked beans, fellas!"

"Nothing's going to stop me from coming along anyway," she said with a sweet smile, though her eyes blazed angrily.

"Only a couple of broken legs," Gary assured her. He turned to address Flynn. "She's not coming as a short-order cook. She'll be an equal team member." His voice lowered. "I'll vouch for her. She's one of the best."

Dana looked at him as he spoke. He had an intense, yet quiet authority to his voice. She was moved. She didn't feel like the image of the strong, competent woman he was painting. Rather, she wanted to be compliant. She wanted him to hold her as he had when he deposited her on Dr. Jenkins' doorstep.

Gary paused so that the full import of his words sank in. "Now, Fairbanks is about one hundred fifty miles to the north of McKinley. We'll charter a snow plane to bring us to Muldrow Glacier and then to bring in the supplies. That should take another two or three trips. We'll spend most of our time, of course, setting up the camps and bringing up reserve supplies. I doubt if we'll be locked in by blizzards or avalanches, but we'll have to make sure we have enough supplies at all points anyway. Given good conditions, I'm hoping for a fast final assault. Any way you look at it, friends, we'll be spending considerable time together in very close quarters. I don't want any personality clashes. Contending with the elements will be hard enough."

His remarks seemed to ease the tension. Dana began to feel almost comfortable as the talk shifted to approaches, historical blunders, equipment, and supplies. From an old-fashioned briefcase that looked like a relic from someone's schooldays, Joe Flynn took out bundles of maps, aerial charts, and equipment manuals.

In order to prevent beer or pop stains from getting on any of the maps, Dana piled the remnants of their lunch on a lucite tray. Just as she bent over to lift it, Gary's strong grip around her forearm stopped her. She looked up into a steady gaze accompanied by an enigmatic smile. The tray shook imperceptibly.

"I'll take that. You study the approaches with Bill and Joe."

Stretching herself out on the floor in front of a large map which Bill and Joe were scrutinizing, she was soon lost in the world she loved best—discussing approaches, balancing distances versus difficulties, and speculating about climatic and ice conditions. Having given the matter

79

much thought before this meeting, she sat hunched over with compass and protractor in an attempt to explain a slightly unorthodox approach that she favored. She was pleased to note that the two men treated her ideas, if not her, with respect.

"LeBlanc, listen to what this gal's got to say," Bill Lewis yelled out.

"I'll be right in," Gary sang out, "as soon as I finish cleaning up in here."

It took the look of amazement that passed between Bill Lewis and Joe Flynn for Gary's words to sink in. Containing a smile and, she had to admit, a touch of guilt, Dana returned to her calculations. A little later her concentration was once more broken, this time by the phone's shrill ring. She heard Gary pick up the receiver.

"Hello." He waited. "Just a minute, ma'am. I'll get her. She's right here on the floor with a couple of mountain climbers." His grin could only be described as wicked as he handed her the phone.

"Yes, Mother." Dana sighed. "No, Mother. That's not what he meant. Please, stop it." She held the phone away from her ear. "I can't talk now, Mother. I'll call you. Yes. That's right. Don't worry. No, Mother, I don't need a porcelain windmill. Yes, I'm sure it's very nice. I have no place to put it." Dana closed her eyes. "Oh, a white Lladro cat. That sounds lovely." Dana tried to put some enthusiasm into her voice. "Why don't you keep it? I have no place for the cat either." Dana rolled her eyes upward. "But actually I don't like porcelain cats. Oh, please, no. Not a Lladro Don Quixote and Sancho Panza!" Dana listened impatiently. "All right, Mother. I'll expect the cat U.P.S. Speak to you next week."

Dana expelled the air that was building up in her lungs.

"Yes, my floor is clean. Don't worry. I promise you, Mother. Nobody is going home with dirty pants. Uh-huh, it's a no-wax floor. You know that. You insisted. Okay. 'Bye, Mother." Hanging up the phone, Dana turned back to the guests, who quickly looked down at the maps with studied nonchalance. "That was my mother," she said.

"Does she climb mountains too?" Lewis asked with a barely disguised smirk.

"No, she's a lion tamer." Dana had to laugh despite herself.

The men chuckled and graciously, she thought, returned to their discussion of routes. The rest of the afternoon was passed in technical discussions. It seemed to Dana that for each of the four of them Mount McKinley represented more than an extremely difficult climb. It was a vindication for every one of life's barbs ever suffered and for every compromise ever made. It was the ultimate climb, the one that would prove beyond the shadow of a doubt the strength and integrity of its conquerors. In the desire to drive themselves to the very edge of what was possible for them, they were all united.

Gary stood up and stretched. He looked at his watch. "It's six o'clock. What do you say we knock it off for today?"

Scrambling to their feet as if they were foot soldiers obeying the commanding officer, Lewis and Flynn thanked Dana for lunch.

"Wait a minute. Let's have a toast before you leave. For good luck." Opening a bottle of cream sherry, Dana filled up four small glasses.

She held hers high, "To Mount McKinley."

"To a successful and exhilarating climb," Lewis chimed in.

"I'll drink to that," Flynn added.

"To us," Gary said as his eyes seemed to Dana to linger disconcertingly on hers.

Clinking glasses, they chugged the smooth amber liquid. The glow of an afternoon's hard work and the toast made palpable a feeling of camaraderie that was quite different from the feeling in her apartment earlier in the day. It was a feeling that was to be short-lived.

"Come on, Gary," Bill prodded when he noticed that their leader made no move to don the jacket that Joe had thrown to him.

"Why don't you go on without me? I've got some things I want to discuss with Dana," Gary said. "I'll catch a cab later on. Here," he tossed his car keys to Bill Lewis.

The look that passed between Bill and Joe as they left her apartment was more eloquent than any words could have been. Once again they relegated her to the status of Gary's mistress.

As the door shut, Dana spun on her heels to face Gary. "What is so important that you had to ruin my hard-won status with your friends?"

"I didn't want to leave yet," he said plainly.

Dana's anger melted at the simple earnestness of his answer. It wouldn't do to let herself believe in a hidden meaning behind his words.

"Well, what did you think of them?" Gary asked, not noticing the tensing of her facial muscles. "Were they as mean and bad as I'd painted them?"

"Yes and no," Dana replied.

"They're good climbers and tough hombres. I think they were impressed with you—with your knowledge of climbing and quick wit, shall we say."

Dana laughed modestly. "What they were impressed with was my lemon mousse."

"That too," Gary said, smiling down at her. "I hope I didn't shock your mother too much."

"You did, but it was good for her. Therapeutic."

He laid a hand on her arm. "You're a strange bird. An enigmatic creature from a land unknown."

"How poetic. Would you like another drink?"

"You know what I'd like." His arms were around her waist. "I'd like your body next to mine and your lips"—he paused to gently part them with his thumb—"on mine."

Dana felt a peculiar, almost unreal thrill pass up her spine as Gary's kiss seemed to melt the boundary between them. The languor she experienced as his hands roamed her back and shoulders and neck made her unwilling to resist his downward pull toward the lush carpet.

Propping himself on his elbow, Gary surveyed her figure with undisguised appreciation and desire. He was about to speak, when Dana knocked his elbow out from under him, resulting in their rolling over each other. Gary ended up on top and kissed her deeply as his strong hands outlined her hips and thighs. Dana moaned softly as Gary hooked his feet against hers and stretched his firm, muscled body along hers, length to length.

As Gary kissed her face and throat and his hands continued to roam her body, Dana reveled in the exquisite sensations her body seemed to radiate. Somewhere in her confused consciousness she even formed the image of herself as a mountain being scaled by this skilled and sensuous mountaineer.

"Oh, Gary," she whispered as he gazed down at her.

"Dana." He pushed her hair back from her face, caressing her cheek in the process. He seemed to hesitate as she shifted position, causing her unbuttoned blouse to fall to the side, exposing her flesh-colored lace bra.

"Is something wrong?" Dana asked.

"Not yet," Gary answered mysteriously as he clasped her hands in his and pulled them above her head. He kissed her hungrily, his tongue delving deep into her mouth. Then suddenly he stopped. "Dana, this isn't right, at least not now it's not."

"I don't understand," she responded.

"It's not appropriate. You'll be on my team, and besides . . ."

"And besides what?"

"Besides nothing." Gary stood and broke the spell Dana realized she'd been in. "Why are you so beautiful?" He paused. "Never mind that. Why do you have all this Lladro around here anyway? It's a little affected, don't you think? I don't understand you, Dana."

"Good. That makes us even, since I can't say you're so transparent either. And as for the Lladro, Mr. LeBlanc, I have it around here because I like it," she lied as she tried to unobtrusively button her blouse.

"Well, to each his own. I just hope you don't carry any in your backpack," Gary answered, appearing to Dana to be uncomfortable and anxious to leave.

Stifling what she wanted to ask and say, Dana continued the pointless bantering between them a few minutes longer until Gary's departure.

CHAPTER FIVE

"Fasten your seat belts, please, and extinguish all cigarettes. We are starting our descent to Fairbanks. The weather is clear, cold, and windy. Hope you all enjoy your stay and make sure to fly back with us."

The stewardess's southern accent was incongruous with the snowy landscape that Dana sighted through the small window. The airplane had been full, with not a seat to spare. That had surprised Dana. Like many mainlanders, she thought that no one went to Alaska unless they had a taste for polar bear meat or for cruises between glaciers.

Her stomach churned. It had been weeks since Gary had left for Fairbanks. And what a send-off! She remembered the incident in her apartment. Had he not decided against it, she surely would have given herself to him. Not a day had passed during these weeks that she had not thought of him and not a night when she had not dreamed of him. Of course his calling almost every day from Fairbanks did not help her to forget him. He started out each conversation with some aspect of the expedition that had to be discussed. He then proceeded to keep her on the phone an additional half hour talking about everything from cars to international politics. The days when he didn't call were disturbingly incomplete.

Over and over she told herself that it was an absurd situation. Two more different people who came from such different worlds, had such different values, could never find common ground. It was a purely physical attraction that existed between them. And anyway, he didn't want her all that much. She tried to convince herself that all she had to do in order to rid her system of him was to phone one of the many men who had pursued her unsuccessfully. But she knew she never would.

Her ears ached from the landing. The gum she chewed to relieve the pressure didn't help. It was only when the plane bumped along the runway that she felt her ears pop. And still she was thinking of Gary. How unlike her this all was. When her mind should be filled with carabiners and pitons, ropes and rucksacks, it was filled instead with him. And she was a woman, she thought ironically, not given to romantic flings or fantasies. So much for knowing oneself!

The plane slowed to a halt. As if someone had yelled fire, Dana unbelted herself, grabbed her belongings, and bolted for the exit. When the door swung open she was going to be the first one out. Her initial glimpse of Alaska would be in the shape of Gary LeBlanc, its first and foremost resident. When she had sent him a telegram with her arrival time he had returned with a call to say he would meet her. It was for that reason that she had chosen with uncharacteristic care her traveling outfit of perilously tight cashmere slacks and sweater. She wanted to look sultry and seductive, she admitted to herself, despite her principles. Anyway, she was tired of the unisex clothing she had been living in lately and which she would be living in again soon. Since Gary had left, Dana had spent almost every day testing specialized snow gear that trapped the body's warmth but which was lightweight and water resistant. It was not attractive clothing, but it was functional. It would help to protect her from one of the greatest dangers—hypothermia, cold stroke. Dana, as well as every ice climber she knew, feared the fall in body temperature, which could drop to as low as eighty-seven degrees. She had long ago memorized the symptoms of hypothermia, where chill and irritability was followed by uncontrollable shivering. She knew that it could be only a matter of minutes before one lapsed into a coma and if not warmed, died. There was one accepted way of preventing death—to be stripped and warmed by another naked body in a sleeping bag. This technique had saved many a life. Hypothermia was one malady Dana did not intend to suffer!

She had also been spending a lot of time perfecting the all-important technique of self-arrest. Not far from where she lived was a sheer snowy cliff which had become her home away from home for six hours a day of intensive practice. Without a rope, she would fall, anchoring her ax into the slope, pressing her chest against its shaft, and digging her toes into the ice to brace herself. After all her practicing, she knew she was ready for this climb.

As the plane door swung open, Dana strode out confidently. It was good to look womanly again and it was good to know that after these weeks of practice she was as proficient a climber as she ever would be. She looked eagerly around the terminal for Gary's power-packed physique. She spotted Bill Lewis's gangly one. Her heart sank.

"Hey, Manchester!" Bill greeted her.

"Hello, Bill." Her voice was subdued. Her eyes scanned the terminal.

"Gary couldn't make it. He asked me to meet you," Bill said quickly, as if guessing her thoughts. "How was your flight?"

"The orange juice tasted like liquefied foam rubber and the smoking section started the row behind mine. It was a good flight."

"You call that a good flight?"

"I'd call a flight bad if I wasn't around to complain about it."

Bill grinned. "I hope you'll keep that sense of humor on McKinley."

Dana smiled weakly. If he only knew what an effort it was to maintain an air of lightness and good humor when her disappointment over Gary's absence burned into her.

Her luggage retrieved, Dana found herself seated beside Bill in Gary's Land-Rover. The sense of humor that Bill had commented on had abandoned her and she found herself, after exchanging news of their respective training programs, with nothing to say. Apparently Bill found himself in the same predicament, for no sooner had he turned on the ignition than he had also turned on the radio at an ear-splitting volume.

She knew she shouldn't jump to conclusions, but she couldn't help but consider the reason Gary hadn't been at the airport to meet her. The reason had to do only with her and with the regret he must feel for having let things go as far as they had. Her forebodings took such hold of her that Dana had no interest in the scenery between the airport and downtown Fairbanks.

"Gary told me to take you to his store before checking you into the hotel," Bill said as he swung down a wide main street.

"If that's what the boss said," Dana retorted.

She noticed the sharp glance Bill threw her way. He knew the reason for her discontent.

Gary's store turned out to be a sporting goods emporium and center for his mountaineering guide service. It was as big as a small department store and had to have every kind of ski, snowmobile, toboggan, and fish hook on the market. For someone who professed disdain for material acquisitions, the owner of this place was quite the entrepreneur, she thought wickedly. Bill signaled to a salesman, who nodded and rushed off. Within moments Gary appeared wearing a wide, welcoming smile.

"Dana, good to see you. Thanks for picking her up, Bill."

She felt like a BLT on toast. Thanks for picking her up indeed, she *harrumphed* to herself.

"Sorry I couldn't meet you. Things are hectic."

"Are you having business problems?" she asked.

"No. This place practically runs itself."

At that moment a pert young woman carrying an attaché case and wearing a dress-for-success pinstripe suit approached him. Without looking at Dana she addressed Gary. "I have the brief prepared. We'll win hands down. There is one problem though. Can we talk?"

"I'll be right with you, Honey," he addressed the young woman. Turning to Dana he spoke off-handedly. "Bill will get you settled. I'll see you later, okay?" He grinned winsomely. "You caught me at a bad time."

"Don't worry about it," Dana said, hearing a sullen note in her own voice.

Gary looked at her sharply. "You tired or something?"

"It's jet lag," Dana excused herself. What should she have expected anyway, she thought, a champagne reception? "Where's Bill?"

"Probably in my office looking at the map. Through that green door." Gary pointed.

In search of Bill, resentment surged through her. To think of the time she had spent imagining this meeting, anticipating it! Her head was held high as she willed away the tears that filled her eyes. She felt an overwhelming need to maintain her dignity. Slowing her pace, she pretended to look over the merchandise as she passed counter upon counter of goods. She imagined his eyes boring into her back, though rationally she knew that they weren't. Nonetheless, she felt a sense of relief as she passed through the heavy green door and out of sight.

Gary's office was paneled in mahogany. It was lit with two hand-crafted stained glass lamps and furnished in leather. One wall was covered with a large relief map of Alaska. In front of that map stood Bill, so engrossed in the geography of the McKinley area that he didn't even turn around at the sound of the door opening.

"You're stuck with me again," Dana said.

"Come here. Take a look at this," Bill said, his eyes still riveted to the map. There followed a lively discussion of possible campsites, which by using mathematical theorems, Bill showed would be safe from avalanches.

The discussion was cut short by Gary's entrance. "Hey, there, Manchester," he said jocularly, "please, forgive me. Something important is in the wind. It couldn't wait. Listen, I have to talk to you." He looked significantly at Bill.

"I'm going," Bill said with what sounded like a snigger.

As the door to the office clicked shut, Gary put his hands on Dana's shoulders. "How do you feel about the environment?"

"What?" she asked.

"How do you feel about the environment?"

"Fine. How do you feel about it?"

"No, I mean it," he insisted.

"That's a strange question," she answered. "The environment? I like it. I like dogs, children, and an environment that's relatively free of sulphuric acid clouds." She made no effort to keep the sarcasm out of her voice.

A lazy smile curved his lips. "Since we agree about the sulphuric acid clouds, the children, and the dogs, how about lending me ten thousand dollars? I'll put up shares in the store as collateral."

"Why do you need it?" A hard knot of suspicion settled in her chest.

"For ecological reasons. Some of us here in Fairbanks are involved in a court case to keep some land from ending up as a dump for chemical waste. That young woman you saw me talking to is our attorney."

"Honey?" Her own tones were honeyed.

"What?" he asked.

"The young woman you called Honey?" she clarified.

"Uh, yes. Honey Moore. She's a bright lawyer and only twenty-four years old. Anyway, we're a little low on funds right now. We need the cash right away and it will take me a couple of days to convert some capital. You'll get your money back as soon we return from the expedition."

A wave of nausea swept over her. "I'll write you a check."

"You'll have the collateral papers this evening," he answered in a businesslike voice.

"No need," she responded brusquely. A voice she recognized as her mother's spoke to her in the back of her mind. Even when they disdain your money they'll use you for it, the voice said. Stick with your own kind if you don't want money to get in the way. Afraid that her mother was right, Dana had rarely used her trust fund. She had lived a simple life. But Gary knew about it. Like a fool she had told him. Perhaps he looked like a god, perhaps he climbed like one, perhaps he even pretended to be one, but this god that was Gary LeBlanc worshipped idols of gold just like every other man she had ever known. He wanted to use her—for her body and her money. That was the simple, crass, ugly truth. If he wanted the ten thousand so badly that he would sacrifice his pride for it, then she would give it to him. Money didn't matter to her. It was only what it stood for that mattered. She would climb the mountain, she would find peace there, and when she came down she would leave Alaska and Gary. And she would learn from the experience.

"I'm glad your trip was all right," Gary said. "I'll have Bill take you to your hotel." He paused a moment, considering. "There's an extra room in my house. You're welcome to use it."

"You mentioned that once before. I declined the generous offer."

He regarded her speculatively. "So you did. I thought perhaps you'd realized that what other people think isn't important. You know you wouldn't have to worry about anything."

"*Anything* is exactly what I wasn't worried about," she answered pointedly.

"You have to be one of the most complex women I've ever met in my life," he chided softly. "The messages you send out all seem to contradict one another. You're hard and soft, cynical and trusting, vulnerable and aloof, sensual but cerebral. Which is the real you?"

"Hard, cynical, aloof, and cerebral," she said stiffly.

"I don't think so," he contradicted her gently.

"Well, you'll never have the opportunity to find out for sure," she taunted. "So you may as well stop trying to solve the puzzle. By the way, you left out one very important adjective in your description of me."

"What's that?" he asked warily.

"Solvent," she snapped.

His face was mottled with rage. "I'm not talking about you physically when I say you're walking a thin line between gross and gorgeous."

"Now, now," she retorted. "How could that line be thin? But let's keep this discussion businesslike. I might as well give you the check now." She opened her purse to fish for her checkbook.

The play of emotions on Gary's face was distinct. Clearly he was waging an inner battle about the money. When he took the check she had scribbled he neglected the common courtesy of a thank-you.

"You'll have the collateral papers delivered to your hotel room shortly," was all he said.

"I told you that wasn't necessary."

"You'll have them. Bill!" he shouted through the door. "You want to take Dana to the Captain Barlett Inn, please? I'll see you back here in an hour." Then he addressed Dana. "We'll meet here tomorrow. A shipment of special goggles just arrived which, I think, will prove superior for our purposes."

With his coolly indifferent tone he froze Dana out of his world. She felt herself shrinking inside herself. She regretted her words to him, regretted what had happened in Boston, regretted that she had ever opened herself up to this man who had no real interest in her, not as a woman. She almost regretted that she had ever heard of this expedition. She had been perfectly content with local climbing. But because she had come this far it did not mean that there was no turning back. If being near Gary became too unpleasant, she always had her return ticket to Boston.

Without warning, her self-control snapped and she felt herself trembling. Her breath caught as she tried to speak. "Is . . . is that all? Am I banished to my hotel room because I dared to question you? Asking someone for ten thousand dollars is not exactly like asking to borrow a buck for a bowl of baked beans!"

"Is that so?" His voice was icy, his stare disdainful. "To me there is no difference. Money is a means to an end, not an end in itself. Since it's so important to you, however, why don't you forget it. You can rip up the check." He fumbled in his back pocket.

Dana felt the color drain from her cheeks. She thought she was going to be sick. "Please, don't. Use the money. I didn't mean it the way it sounded. I know it's for a good cause."

With a harsh sigh he raked his fingers through his thick hair. "If this were for my personal use for any reason whatsoever, I wouldn't touch it. I wouldn't go near it!" He was vehement. "But with so much at stake," he said resignedly, "it wouldn't be fair for me to follow my inclinations."

Her fists were clenched stiffly at her sides. "I don't want to argue about money. Money. I've been trying to get rid of its curse my whole life. But it haunts me. Believe me. It's not the money I care about. It's just . . ."

"What?" He laughed mirthlessly. "Do you think I'm a fortune hunter? Rest assured, my pretty, I'm not a hunter at all."

Had he slapped her with the back of his hand she would have reeled no more than from his words. They struck her with cruel forcefulness. He wasn't interested in her. It had all been a delusion on her part. What a fool he must think her! No greater a fool than she thought herself, after assessing the situation.

"I'll see you in the morning, Dana." He strode toward the door and paused, his hand on the knob to look over his shoulder at the stricken face of the woman he had allowed to insinuate herself into his life. "LeBlanc's folly," he muttered and left.

Dana stood still as a statue. What had he meant by that? That he had made a mistake in letting her come? That was clear to her as well as to him. Why did everything have to be complicated by sex and money? Why couldn't Gary have considered her neutrally as the good climber she was? Why did he have to wonder how she would be in his bed? Women's liberation. Hah!

Bill, his pale blond looks blending in with the snowy landscape, was back to escort her to the hotel. The Captain Barlett Inn where Gary had reserved a room for her was comfortable, lacking the sterility of so many hotel rooms, which cheered her up somewhat.

"Do you want a little guided tour of the city?" Bill offered awkwardly. "I've been here a few days, so I can show you around."

"No thanks, Bill. I want to get settled."

As soon as her door clicked shut Dana sat down on the

edge of her bed. Almost immediately she jumped up. She wouldn't let despair claim her! She wouldn't let him get to her! Goodness knows, while climbing she wouldn't be thinking about him. If she thought about anything other than the next hand- or foothold, it would be the last thing she would ever think about. So she might as well condition her mind to ignore Gary LeBlanc except in his role as team leader. Since Fairbanks was known as the Golden Heart of Alaska, she might as well see a bit of it. And she would do it on her own.

Teeming Fairbanks was the state's second largest city. Dana soon lost herself in the vibrant downtown section. Many of the historic turn of the century buildings with their round turrets bespeaking Alaska's Russian influence struck her fancy. Though the shops with their walrus tusks, rough gold nuggets, and polar bear skins looked enticing, she resisted the urge to browse and wandered instead to the still frozen Tanana River. Passing close to a knot of old-timers who were arguing, she listened in. They were taking bets on the date the river would thaw! She walked on.

Fairbanks, with its university that housed a world-famous archeological museum and with its native trappers' camps where you could see fur caches and fish drying on racks, was a study in contrasts. It was a city that showed the effects of two major bursts of growth. The first was the turn of the century gold rush. The second was when Fairbanks became the major rail and highway connection to the Trans-Alaskan Pipeline.

As interesting as the city was, Dana strolled with only half a mind on it. Her gaze constantly turned to the north, where from one hundred fifty miles away she could see Mount McKinley hunched against the sky like an enormous polar bear. What she really wanted to do was to board a motor coach to Denali National Park for her first close-up glimpse of the mountain. She had had enough travel for one day, however.

Her first impressions of Alaska could be described only in superlatives, she thought as dusk descended. The people were the friendliest. The few times she had asked directions of passersby they had each offered to escort her to her destination and had given her tips on their city. The vistas were the most breathtaking. The promise of adventure rang pure and true.

The next two days were busy ones. There were last minute equipment changes and always there was more discussion. After what seemed to Dana to be endless talk they finally compromised on what to take in the small, plastic medical kits each of them would carry. They agreed on headache pills, anti-diarrhea medication, altitude sickness pills, ampoules of penicillin, and pills for the prevention of pulmonary edema, a form of pneumonia and one of the deadliest of illnesses that can affect the climber.

The average team took about twenty days to climb McKinley, though one well-known mountaineer had miraculously accomplished it in one day. Gary planned one week for the climb, an impressive feat if they were to do it. Unlike many mountaineers, neither Gary nor Dana, Bill nor Joe, were driven by the desire to be first. McKinley had been climbed several times before. They could always find one of the unnamed Matterhorn-like peaks in Alaska to climb first, but that was not important to them. What mattered was doing the climb well, doing it quickly, and enjoying nature's peace.

On the morning they were to set out for Muldrow Glacier from which they would begin their ascent, Dana found herself in Gary's office alone with him for the first time since the incident with the ten thousand dollars.

"Cup of coffee?" he asked as he poured her a mug of the steaming brew.

"Thank you." As she took the coffee from him his fingers brushed against her palm. She started, acutely conscious of his rough, callused skin, and as she did so, her eyes rose to his. He was staring at her with a look of desire so naked and burning, it was unmistakable. She felt as if her suddenly weak legs would buckle under her. To her surprise, he stepped away, as if from something dangerous. As he turned toward his desk she saw the constrained smile that twisted his lips. She ran her tongue nervously along her dry lower lip.

"Did you get an up-to-date weather report yet?" she asked.

"Clear, cold, and dry. The snow plane will pick us up in an hour and a half."

"Shouldn't we get going to the airport?" Dana asked nonchalantly.

"The pilot will wait. We're his only passengers," Gary said impassively though a grin softened the hard lines of his uncompromising features. "How do you feel? Are you excited?" His eyes raked her from head to toe as he asked, though why, Dana couldn't tell, for her layers of weatherproof garments disguised both curves and planes, making her feel as attractive as an Egyptian mummy.

"Sort of," Dana replied.

"You're exciting," Gary said with his old twinkle. "You're excited and you're exciting. That's a combination hard to beat. But I don't know how well it will work as we hop from one wafer-thin foothold to the next."

"Is this to be a recurrent theme throughout the climb?"

Dana flashed. "If you're not sure of me, it's not too late to change your mind. I can always take a Cook's cruise of the inside passage instead. Maybe I'll change my mind if you don't," she threatened. "I'm quite tired of being doubted and baited."

"And used?" he asked with an ominous glint to his eyes.

"Maybe." She tossed her head defiantly.

"How feminine a gesture for so unfeminine a character," he taunted. "How feisty you are and how tired you must be of it."

"You're quite right," she snapped sarcastically. "Like any woman in her right mind, my real goal is to be like Donna Reed. I'm just looking for the right man to bring slippers to. Meanwhile I'm putting in my time climbing mountains. You know, this might have been a big mistake. None of you really wants me along."

Gary shrugged. "I recommend that you take care then that nobody clips your rope."

"Very funny," she said lamely, aware that she deserved the jibe. "Anything happen on that ecology case you were involved with?" She bit her tongue. Why had she brought that up? He would think she was referring to the money again.

"We're sitting tight. You have the collateral agreement put in a secure place, I presume?"

"It's in the hotel safe," she answered. "What's your part in this whole thing? I never did get it straight."

"I'm interested in old Mother Earth. Where in tarnation are Bill and Joe?"

"Maybe they overslept," Dana said flippantly, knowing full well that if they were anything like her they had trouble getting any sleep last night.

"Hmm." Gary was absorbed in a last-minute check of his pack.

"Don't forget your dictionary of insults in case the well runs dry," Dana advised.

"No chance of the well drying up," he answered. "Not with the opportunities you provide."

"I asked for that, didn't I?" she said ruefully. "Let's call a truce, at least until the climb is over."

"No need," he grinned wickedly. "We'll be much too busy to insult each other, or even to think of each other."

"Do we think of each other?" she asked haltingly, suspended halfway between a defensive disbelief and tenderness.

"I think so." With an unexpected wistfulness he brushed the hair that had fallen across her cheek behind her ear.

Once again she was conscious only of the touch of his fingers on her hair, her face, tracing the line of her jaw. And once more she saw the devouring flame behind his cool gaze.

Raucous laughter floated into the office through the half open door. Bill Lewis and Joe Flynn entered carrying grocery bags.

"We stopped at the store," Joe said, "for some very important provisions." He displayed the contents of his bag which was filled with biodegradable toilet tissue.

"We already have that packed," Gary said.

"Better too much than too little," Joe explained. "If we ran out, it wouldn't be comfortable having to use a flat slab of ice." He guffawed.

Gary shook his head disapprovingly at Joe's crassness. "You're in the company of a lady, Flynn."

A scowl darkened Joe Flynn's brow.

He was about to say something when Dana interjected, "Please, it's all right. Don't feel that you have to censor yourself on my account."

Irrationally, Joe's scowl deepened. He was manifestly put out by the rebuke.

"My bag's got the good stuff," Bill said. He held up a Baby Ruth candy bar in each hand. "I've got Mounds, Cadbury, Hershey's, Nestlé's, marzipan, and red licorice. Not to mention Chuckles, jelly beans, and coconut patties. How's that for thoughtfulness? Hey? What do you say, guys? Where's the round of applause? You're going to be so grateful when that wind's whistling around you in the black glacial night and you've still got to consume two thousand more of that daily six thousand calories we'll need and you're sick to death of liverwurst. It will seem like the world's coming to an end, and then . . . you'll bite into a bar of Nestlé's! You'll know whom to thank!" His forced jocularity eased the tension that had been so thick just a couple of minutes earlier.

"I love Nestlé's Crunch," Dana babbled. She felt as if she had been punched in the stomach. Joe was clearly hostile toward her. Gary's hostility was masked by his sexual come-on, and Bill acted as if Dana were some weird specimen who had to be humored. All of them would be happier if she just disappeared, she thought morosely. On the other hand, Gary had just defended her against what he perceived as an insult. Dana felt that she should have been amused and touched. Vulgarity didn't offend her. It was so pervasive that she had learned to shrug it off. What really offended her was insensitivity and materialism. Gary did not understand her.

"On the morning before this much-planned expedition

it's a little odd to be standing around discussing candy bars," Gary observed.

Dana, still shaken from the near blow-up with Joe, made a stab at levity. "We shouldn't be discussing anything. We should be saying some ancient Eskimo prayers to ward off avalanches, frostbite, and bickering!"

"Dana's right," Gary supported her. "If we start quarreling now, God help us when a blizzard traps us for a couple of days in the same tent."

Dana looked at him askance, feeling a warm flush spread slowly over her face. He had defended her two times in a row. Could he be having a change of heart? Could she? Frantically she tried to remember how much he irritated her.

"You sure it's wise, Dana, to put yourself in a tent with three guys?" Joe asked with a weasel-like leer in what was clearly a last-ditch effort to dissuade her.

"Careful, Flynn," Gary warned in an ominously low voice. "One more crack like that and you'll be nursing a left hook in the jaw." A vein pulsed in Gary's forehead and his face tensed. There was a primitive expression in his glistening eyes.

A feeling of being manipulated descended upon Dana and she wanted to shout her defiance at both men—at Joe for his obnoxiousness, but especially at Gary for maneuvering her into the position of helpless female. They reminded her of two prehistoric animals, or maybe blind rhinos locking horns in combat.

"I can take care of myself, thank you," she addressed Gary. "As for you, Joe, I may as well tell you that besides mountaineering and"—she paused for emphasis—"Lladro, I have a fondness for karate, *and* a brown belt!" She paused to dramatize the lie.

102

Joe Flynn flashed her a sickly smile and nodded moodily.

There was mockery in Gary's eyes but all he said was, "After a day's climb I doubt if any of us will have enough energy to play tiddledywinks. Let's leave sexual politics back here in civilization along with the dirt, noise, and pollution."

"There's not too much of that in Fairbanks," Bill said.

Dana smiled shallowly and astonished herself by saying, "There is in this office."

"In that case this will be the last time the four of us gather here," Gary said grimly.

His gaze was fiercely protective though he clearly attempted, for the good of the expedition, to temper what seemed to Dana to be a ridiculously macho reaction to Joe. One would think, thought Dana, that he had more at stake here than simply maintaining harmony among the four climbers. And they said women were hard to figure out!

"I'll be back in ten minutes," Dana said abruptly. "I want to walk around the block."

The clean, brisk air slapped at her cheeks, clearing her mind somewhat. Still she wavered. Why was she doing this climb? She toted up a list of the pros and cons of the expedition. As usual with such lists, however, it did little but accentuate her indecisiveness. Her overriding feeling was that she was never more at peace, never more in harmony with herself and the world than when she was climbing. Her overriding fear was that the clash of personalities and the animosity engendered by her sex would poison the serenity of the mountain.

Spotting a pay phone, Dana gave in to impulse and called her mother in Scarsdale. "Hello, Mother."

"Dana, is that you? Are you calling from Mount McKinley?"

"No, Mother," Dana answered patiently. "There are no phones on Mount McKinley. We're just about to leave Fairbanks though. How are you?"

"I'm fine. It's you I'm worrying about. Don't forget to wear a sweater under your coat and a warm cap. Are you sure those three men are gentlemen? I don't like the idea of it."

"I'll be fine," she said wearily, though the first three minutes were not yet up.

Her mother's voice pierced across the thousands of miles of telephone wire. "I don't know why you want to go to Alaska and climb around on glaciers, for heaven's sake. It's so dangerous, I çan't bear to think of it. Imagine, dangling by a thin little rope miles on high! There are so many lovely things you could be doing if you would move back here with us. There's a marvelous opening at Studio One of miniature porcelains and there's a whole string of June parties coming up. There's never a dull moment around here. And for exercise, there's a new slimming salon in town. I know you don't need slimming, dear, but I do know how you like to keep active. And you could stop doing those dreadful push-ups. You know, muscles are really quite unattractive on a young woman. And you must take care that with all your climbing your thighs don't get too thick." Her mother's voice lowered conspiratorially. "You know, dear, I just read that thick thighs mean too much testosterone in a woman's system! That's the male hormone, you know!"

Dana heard a familiar smugness in her mother's voice. She could tell that she had been dying to impart that choice bit of information.

"Thanks for telling me, Mother. Look, you take care and give my love to Dad. I've got to hurry along now. We're leaving any minute and I've still got to shave!"

Dana chuckled as she heard mother's gasp before hanging up. For some reason her mother's total ignorance of her passion and her inane responses—could she really think there were phones on Mount McKinley or that Dana would forget her "cap"—did not annoy her or make her angry. Curiously it helped her resolve her indecision about the trip.

Her determination intact, she nevertheless felt a tear and then another trickle down her cheek as she headed back toward the store. Disillusionment swamped her. She had known that she would meet with opposition from this crew, but she hadn't known that she would be so absurdly hurt by it. What had she done to earn their contempt? And why had Gary chosen her to come along if he was still thinking of her as a woman first and a mountaineer second?

She was beginning to take a jaundiced view of her skirmishes with Gary. When first they had met she had thought it would be merely an irritation. Now she found that she was affected by his disturbing presence when she was with him and when she was alone. How ironic that she climbed for the peace and beauty of it and now, faced with the most challenging and potentially rewarding climb of her life, she found herself in a turmoil of conflicting emotions.

Dana tightened at the sound of footsteps approaching. Stepping beside her, his face deadly serious, Gary stopped her. Without a word he brushed at her tear-stained cheeks. Her pulse leaped, and where her cheeks had been wet now they burned. She felt the velvety brown of his eyes caressing her, probing the secrets of her soul. Dana remained rigid, willing her heart to stop its insane racing and her knees to stop their shaking. If on the imminent climb she didn't have better control of her responses, she would be either dead or grounded on the glacier. But, she thought quickly, it seemed that she was more vulnerable to this man than she had been to anyone or anything before. If Mount Rainier, if the Black Dike, if the White Mountains, could not defeat her, it seemed that Gary LeBlanc could!

"No tears," he said kindly. "You're a full and equal partner in this expedition. Don't let some thoughtless words hurt you. They, or should I say we, respect you more than you think."

His strong arms draped about her, Dana swayed against his lean body. "I was just talking to my mother. She reminded me to wear a warm cap," Dana laughed.

"You look even more beautiful when you laugh." He looked at her intently. "Let's load our gear."

As if a bright sun had penetrated a gloomy fog, Dana's spirits soared and her anticipation redoubled. This would be a wonderful climb after all!

Back at his office the atmosphere, though it had only been a matter of ten or fifteen minutes since she had left, was noticeably more cordial.

By way of apology Joe, who had emptied Bill's bag of candy in a pile on the floor, offered first choice of rations to Dana. Much to her surprise, he even helped her on with her pack. The weight took getting used to, though her pack was a mere forty pounds, trivial compared to the staggering eighty-five-pound packs the men were to carry. In addition there were many supplies that were to be airlifted to the glacier and taken up in relays to the three camps at various elevations that they had to establish before attempting the summit. In that way, were they to be faced with weather conditions that made the assault impossible for a time, they would never be too far from safety.

As they were about to leave, a salesclerk rapped impatiently at Gary's door. Entering, he announced excitedly that a shipment of nonrefundable inflatable rafts had just been returned from a store in Chicago and what should he do? Gary shrugged wearily, saying he would take care of it upon his return.

"Getting and spending we lay waste our powers," he quoted the immortal line of Wordsworth.

Dana agreed wholeheartedly as she checked the time on her platinum waterproof, shockproof, tastefully diamond-studded Cartier watch. "If people only knew how little the glitter which we surround ourselves with means."

She didn't notice the quizzically raised eyebrows of the three men who had so recently agreed to bridge the gap between them.

CHAPTER SIX

Having unpacked their equipment and provisions on Muldrow Glacier, all the trivia of ordinary life seemed to melt away, leaving only clean air, snow, and mountains. Dana sensed that the others felt this, too, since they all went about their duties wordlessly like contented monks. The only sounds were the lap dogs Gary had hired to sled provisions up to the lowest ridge. Past that point they'd be on their own.

Though people most often thought of ropes, pitons, and death-defying acrobatics when they thought of mountain climbing at all, more than half the battle of climbing a peak such as McKinley was in the establishment of intermediate camps. The bring-up of reserve supplies was, though routine, quite essential. Without the camps, any little mishap would result in an aborted mission or a dangerously rapid descent so as to return before starvation or exposure set in.

Daily reconnoitering was another of the pre-assault

routines that had to be undertaken. By some sort of unspoken mutual consent the reconnoitering missions were generally broken up into two parties: Joe with Bill, and Dana with Gary. From the men's point of view Dana knew this pairing was logical—the strongest with the weakest and the two intermediate members together. Despite their words of good faith, Dana knew full well that Joe and Bill, at least, were still not convinced of her expertise.

On the morning of their second day Dana found herself skiing along the glacier with Gary. They were enroute to find a safe spot for the establishment of their second camp. That meant a spot relatively protected from the threat of avalanches and falling rock. Joe and Bill stayed at the first camp because they were both experiencing some slight vertigo and thought they should take it easy.

Even through the thick, protective sunscreen which she wore, Dana felt the sun's rays burning into her face, and her eyes even with the tinted goggles she wore were strained from the glare of the snow.

"You'd better put on your ski mask," Gary advised her, clearly suffering from the same malady, "or that peaches and cream complexion you have is going to look like prunes and jelly by the end of this expedition."

Dana laughed. "You, too, or you might look like an overboiled hot dog."

"I love these romantic conversations." Gary winked back at her.

"Look at that orange sun and those red clouds," Dana said in an awe-inspired voice. "Doesn't it make you feel like you're in another world?"

"It's the closest thing on earth to being on the moon,"

Gary said with the same sense of awe. "I'm glad we're here."

She felt an extra sense of buoyancy at his words, which she tried to camouflage with her monotone. "You are?"

"Sure," he answered breezily. "It's a long way from the Oak Bar at the Plaza."

She stiffened slightly. "Over there looks like a good spot to plant the flag." She pointed to a flat area with no noticeable avalanche scars nearby.

Gary yawned as he squinted toward the area.

"I thought you slept well last night," she remarked.

"I did," he said, "except when the polar bear bit my toe. To tell you the truth, I'm feeling a little headachy."

"So am I," she answered. "Altitude sickness must be getting to us."

"Maybe it's love sickness," he teased, lunging for her playfully.

The tangle of their skis prevented them from coming together or from moving apart. Trying to disentangle themselves, they tumbled in an ungainly manner in the snow. "Looks like we've fallen for each other," he smirked.

Wordlessly she packed a perfectly round snowball and aimed it at his shoulder. Just as wordlessly Gary removed his skis and dove on top of Dana.

"Listen, woman. On second thought, don't listen. We talk too much." His mouth descended on hers and tenderly demanded a response. She squirmed against him, moving her face away, denying to him and to herself the sparks that his kiss had ignited, sparks that contrasted with the icy landscape.

"Don't," she moaned, sitting halfway up, searching for

110

a way to alter the fact that this ill-fated passion was slowly consuming her. "You're smearing my ChapStick."

"Will words never fail you?" he laughed, her joke taking the edge off their desire. "I shouldn't have done that. It was unprofessional."

"It seemed very professional to me," she answered. "Or at least like a well-practiced amateur."

"I suppose you have quite a basis of comparison," he rejoined.

Her ardor turned to annoyance. "It's my climbing ability that's your concern, not my morals! And whatever basis for comparison I have, it's quite likely that you have more!" She refastened her skis hurriedly.

"Dana," he said ominously. "Dana," he called again.

"What?" She looked up in time to get a powdery snowball flush in her face. "What kind of response was that?" she asked, half frowning, half smiling.

"With you, nonverbal responses are best. I'm learning not to cross tongues with you, at least not in that way."

"I thought we got all that straightened out in Fairbanks. When are you going to put an end to these sexual overtones?"

"When the snow melts on Mount McKinley," he answered glibly. "Lighten up. Can't you take a joke, Manchester? We've got a lot of serious work ahead of us. You're right about that area you pointed out a little while ago. It looks fine for the camp."

Together they skied over to the ridge surrounding it, where they took off their skis, put on their crampons, and roped up. The climbing was not especially difficult, though it was time-consuming. Gary had to dig out every foothold with his ax and plant ice screws for the rope anchor. It took twenty minutes or more to move a few feet. When they arrived at the well-protected stretch of flat ground Gary removed his banner from his pack, which he planted in the ground as a marker.

"G.L.," she read his initials as the banner unfurled in the wind. "I wouldn't say that's egocentric, would you?"

He grinned wickedly. "G marks the spot!"

She shot him a sharp glance.

When they returned to base several hours later, Joe had dinner steaming on the propane stove. It was a stew made from freeze-dried pork, beans, and potatoes. Dana forced herself to finish her portion, though she declined seconds. While the others shoveled forkfuls of the grayish concoction into their mouths, Dana busied herself by melting snow for instant coffee.

"Better make that Sanka," Joe advised.

"Sanka it is," Dana agreed. "We need our sleep. I can hardly believe that in two more days we start the final assault. I feel as if I've lost all sense of time. It almost seems as if time has stopped and we're suspended here in this icy dimension."

"Yeah," said Joe, characteristically eloquent.

"Not only does time seem slowed down," said Gary, "but all my senses are heightened—sight, hearing, smell, touch." He looked at Dana.

She felt herself growing uneasy. "How about taste?"

Gary looked down at his empty bowl of stew. "That, too, unfortunately."

Bill, absorbed in a book of computer programs, was oblivious to the conversation.

Dana glanced at the cover of Bill's book. "Why are you reading that? Isn't getting away from the world of numbers and words and details one of the reasons you climb?"

Bill spoke solemnly. "The purity of some of these programs is comparable in its own way to the purity of mountain climbing. I see no contradiction."

"That's interesting," Dana replied, not quite understanding what he meant but glad that he had taken her question seriously.

"Besides," Bill continued, "who says there are no numbers or details connected with climbing, at least with serious climbing. God knows there have been with this climb, and you've been involved with all of them."

"I guess so," Dana agreed, musing at the new light Bill's comments seemed to shed on matters. Still, she insisted silently to herself that reading a book on computer programming up here seemed a little weird.

"What are you doing, LeBlanc?" Joe growled inquisitively.

"Whittling," Gary answered as he turned over a block of ice on the floor of the boxlike tent.

Dana, whose own curiosity had been aroused at Gary's actions, was pleased that someone else had asked.

"Whittlin' what?" Joe pursued with his peculiar economy of words.

"A hand," Gary answered, his attention focused on the ice.

"An ice sculpture!" Dana exclaimed, her eyes opened wide. "I didn't know you could sculpt! Is that a special tool you're using?"

"Uh-huh. An Eskimo friend of mine showed me how to do this." His brow was furrowed in concentration. "I'm trying to do something along the lines of that Lladro sculpture you're so fond of. The only problem with mine is that you have to keep it in the freezer."

"That's probably where I should keep my Lladro." Dana laughed gaily.

113

At that, the three men looked at her in puzzlement.

"I have to admit," she gave a shy laugh, "I hate that Lladro stuff. Your sculpture shows a lot more warmth, despite its temperature."

"Why the huffy defense of it in your apartment?" Gary wondered aloud.

"For the same reason that a person can make all sorts of unpleasant but true observations about their mother, father, son, daughter, dog, cat, parakeet, or Lladro, but heaven help the stranger who says the same thing."

"I'm a stranger?"

"You were then," Dana smiled. Aware of becoming too personal, she added for the benefit of the rest of the team, "I couldn't call anyone a stranger with whom I've gotten so high!"

They all chuckled and Bill, diverted from his book, even threw in a one-liner. "We're an upwardly mobile group."

Dana was warmed, feeling like one of the team.

Joe swallowed a handful of vitamins with his Sanka. "I'm going to try out these prevention pills for pulmonary edema," he said.

Gary shrugged. "What for? We're still too low to worry about that."

"I figure it's better to try these pills out now than when we're nearing the summit. What if they have some strange side effects?"

"If you want to be a human guinea pig, suit yourself," Bill said. "I never thought we should bring that medicine along. Not enough is known about it. I personally don't know anyone who has taken it. I don't care what medical research says."

"Spoken like a true scientist," Gary teased him good-naturedly.

Gary had himself been unsure about those pills, including them at the last minute. "Just don't become a hypochondriac now," he cautioned Joe. "You seemed pretty concerned about that dizzy spell you had and now you're worrying about pulmonary edema."

"Yeah," Joe answered sarcastically. "What's a little pneumonia among friends?" Despite his words he looked embarrassed as he unscrewed the cap on the pills.

"Looking at you one would never think you were the worrying sort," Dana observed. "You're the picture of vitality."

"We'll be learning a lot about one another in the next several days," Gary said, his face imperturbable as he sat cross-legged before his burgeoning hand of ice.

"Say, LeBlanc." Joe prodded Gary with a finger. "If these pills turn out to be funny or something, get me one of your hotshot lawyer friends to handle the case. A good settlement and I'll cut you a slice."

Gary didn't look at Joe as he answered. "You know, my friend, I don't do that kind of thing."

"Right," Joe muttered. "You're pure. You and Lewis. I suppose it's like getting religion."

Though the sound of Gary's chiseling remained constant, there was a testiness to his tone, his demeanor, to his posture even. "I don't answer to anyone, Flynn. That's how I want it."

Dana had been rooted to the floor of the tent listening to the exchange between the two men. It was an exchange that raised questions for her. What, really, was Gary like? She couldn't hazard a guess.

The fumes of the butane stove smarted her eyes. Pulling herself to her feet, she hunched over and exited through the flap of the boxlike tent. The night landscape was lit by

115

a red moon that made the ice peaks and spires glow eerily. The strange and beautiful ice formations on the glacier took on lifelike shapes. It was much like the phenomenon of looking at clouds or stars and seeing pictures in them, except that this, so close by, could have been quite scary had she let her imagination run away with her. The silence was total; the cold was so sharp it took a minute before she felt it. If, as she thought, she had wanted to escape the unfriendly barbs that had so quickly poisoned the atmosphere, she soon realized that unanswered questions were much preferable to unbearable cold.

Upon reentering the tent, she was struck by the fumes of the butane stove and the greasy odor of leftover stew. She picked up the pot. "Anybody want to finish this? If not, I'm throwing the rest out."

"Waste not, want not," Joe reproached her. "Someone might have a yen for it in the morning."

Dana wrinkled her nose. "I am not sleeping with this stench!"

Rousing himself from his whittling, Gary smiled lopsidedly. "She's right, Flynn, and anyhow, you know the wealthy are unaware of the travails of a base-camp cook!" He took the pot from Dana and emptied it outside. When he returned, instead of gray mush it was filled with snow, which he would melt in order to clean it.

Although Dana recognized Gary's remark as good-natured ribbing, it irked her. She twisted her mouth mockingly. "You're quite right, Gary. If they don't like the odor of freeze-dried stew, let them sniff Arpege!" With that she flipped open her backpack and withdrew the small atomizer of perfume that she had impulsively brought. Spraying it into the air, she breathed deeply.

"Ahhh."

"Yechh!" Joe groaned.

"And let them eat cake!" Bill laughingly added, taking out an aluminum pan of brownies from the supplies.

Dana noticed Gary watching her, a strange smile on his face. When their eyes met he stood up, placed his ice sculpture outside, and moved over to her. Languidly he sank onto her air mattress, ostensibly to have better access to the pan of brownies. Although she told herself it was silly, his nearness made her wary and nervous. She was all too aware of the pungent male scent of him, despite the Arpege in the air. His was a scent that appealed to her, she realized with horror, more than that of French perfumes. With Gary she felt as if she were hovering on the brink, almost as if with one small misstep she would plunge off the face of the mountain.

"Anybody want to play gin rummy?" Joe asked. "No takers? I'll play solitaire then," a promise he proceeded to carry out and which kept him occupied for the remainder of the evening.

Once again Bill buried himself in his book. That left Dana and Gary still sitting side by side.

Noticing a slight tremble in her hand as she reached for a brownie, Gary asked softly, "Are you frightened?"

She turned her head angrily in his direction. How dare he continue in this vein in the presence of the other two men? And how arrogant, how egotistical! "You're not the sort of man who frightens me," she stated as evenly as she could. "I've known others like you. They've all been paper tigers."

The menace in his taut features was fleeting, but it lasted long enough to send shivers up and down her spine. It was replaced with an expression of lazy, wry, placating humor. "I wasn't talking about me, you ninny. I was referring to the assault the day after tomorrow. In case you forgot, that *is* the reason we came up here."

Embarrassment washed over her in waves. Though there was no indication that the others had heard, she wished at that moment that she could disappear off the face of the earth, or at least off the face of the mountain. "Don't worry. I haven't forgotten." More loudly, "I think you'd better move now. I'm going to sleep. Good night, everyone." Unlike in more civilized climates, not to mention the unusual social climate, she added clothes rather than took them off. When the sun went down, the cold was penetrating and absolute.

Racked by thoughts of her disturbing encounters with Gary, Dana's sleep was fitful. What made it worse was her awareness of Joe's hourly need to leave the tent. Finally, after many hours of tossing and turning and wondering what Joe was like after attending a beer party, she slept.

Although her eyes were red-rimmed when she awoke, she was positively bushy-tailed compared to Joe, whose color could have allowed him to blend in with the landscape. Neither Gary nor Bill appeared to take much notice of Joe's state. After her misunderstanding with Gary the previous night, Dana was hesitant about making waves. When Joe went outside the tent again, Dana realized she could not keep quiet. This was serious business and it was essential that every member of the team be in tiptop shape for the safety of the entire team. Joe was grinning sheepishly when he came back inside the tent.

"Okay," Gary said. "Everything set?" Aware that as they climbed higher it would take longer and longer to get themselves started each morning, Gary was anxious to start out quickly. This would be the last time they would keep regular hours, in any case, for most of their climbing was to be done at night.

Dana took a deep breath. She looked Joe straight in the eye and spoke loudly and deliberately. "Joe, you're in no shape to work on Camp Three today. I was up and I know how you were last night."

Joe looked at her balefully. "It's nothing."

"What's going on?" Gary asked. "You sick, Joe?"

"Nah, nothing serious."

Dana licked her dry lips. "I think it was more than that. I read the information booklet that came with those pills you took, Joe. Did you?" Joe maintained a stony silence. "The possible side effects include polyuria. You were up all night going to the bathroom. The way that medicine works is by dehydrating the body. With less bodily fluid there's less chance of fluid going to the lungs. By the way, do you realize the illness this medication prevents is quite rare? And that it will deplete your body of the one and a half gallons of liquid you're supposed to drink daily on a climb like this?"

"Thank you, Dr. Manchester," Joe muttered.

"No charge," she said sweetly. "Just stay off those pills for a day and you'll be fine."

Gary made a firm decision. "The assault will take place one day later. Bill and I will spend the day moving equipment to Camp Three so that when we start tomorrow it will be with light packs. Dana, if you were up listening to Joe last night, you can't be in such great shape yourself. Take it easy. Bill and I can take care of it by ourselves."

"And me?" Joe asked.

"You stay here with the doc," Gary said, smiling at both of them.

Later, outside the tent, Dana whispered to Gary, "Shouldn't my punishment fit the crime?"

"It does, my dear," Gary whispered back as he unexpectedly ran his finger down the side of Dana's face and then softly pushed her hair back over her shoulder. Suddenly he grasped her and pulled her to him. "Leaving you here is my punishment." He kissed her tenderly and then when Dana was about to speak, he covered her with kisses again. Hearing Bill approach, Gary whispered, "Let's just pretend you've already said something nasty and there's no need to say it again. Have a nice day."

"But, but . . ." Dana stammered. "What will I do here?"

"Call your mother." Gary winked.

CHAPTER SEVEN

The day was spent uneventfully, trying to make small talk with Joe and sorting out her feelings about Gary. Why had he kissed her? Why did he say that being away from her would be punishment for him? Why did he contradict himself so often when it came to her? What did he want from her? What did she want from him? The crystal-clear mountain air was not having its customary calming effect on her.

When Gary and Bill returned late that afternoon they were too tired to talk. By four in the afternoon all of them were sound asleep. The real climbing was more safely done at night to minimize the likelihood of ice melting and falling off in chunks. They planned to start out at two A.M. for Camp Three. Since almost everything they would need was already up there, the packs would be blissfully light.

"Cut it out," Gary good-naturedly warned Bill, who was shadow-boxing, throwing punches into the snow. Besides, Bill, Dana and Joe also seemed relieved that the expedition was finally off the ground, so to speak. "Come on, you're going to need all that energy to get to Three in reasonable shape."

"I like the old rope better than this fancy one," Joe muttered. "When this gets wet it's so slick you can't hold on and when you do you get ice burns."

Rolling her eyes, Dana wondered why Joe saw fit to complain now. It was a beautiful clear peaceful night with the sky full of twinkling stars. "That was a bitter cup of coffee you made back there at camp, Bill," Joe complained again. "I need a good mellow cup to start me off. Next time you should be in charge of the coffee, Dana."

"Sorry. I don't do windows or coffee," she said dryly. She remembered what Gary had told her the first time they had met, that he had climbed once with two women and they had complained too much. They couldn't have been much worse than Joe, she thought.

As if on cue, Joe groaned about his headache. As they continued their horizontal trek along the glacier, Dana's eyes met Gary's. His conspiratorial smile indicated to her that he knew what she was thinking.

The glacier was treacherous only when covered with snow that hid its deep crevasses. This year most of the snow had melted early, leaving sizeable stretches of gray-blue pulverized rock. For that reason they decided not to rope up along the glacier. That, it turned out, was a mistake.

They came to an area that couldn't have been more than twenty yards across, covered by knee-deep slush. The consistency reminded Dana of those flavored Sno Cones that give you an instant headache if you're foolhardy enough to take a big sip without first warming it in your mouth.

The going was difficult, each step requiring great effort. Dana had pushed forward, taking the lead with Gary's tacit approval. Taking the lead was something she would never be permitted to do on an ascent. But here, she figured, she could push snow aside as well as the next person could. Since she had so much less to carry than the others she thought it only fair that she take on this laborious task of pushing aside the snow with her legs.

She jammed her feet and her knees into the slush, pushing ahead slowly but steadily. A sense of wonder overcame her, for the white areas of the glacier seemed to shimmer in the moonlight. Glancing up, she gazed at the summit which was barely visible. It appeared to her as remote and otherworldly.

Wonderment at the spectacular vista stayed with her as she quickened her pace, anxious not to lose time. Then suddenly where her foot should have met hard snow it met soft, airy snow, and before she knew what was happening to her, her hands were flailing, her feet were twitching, and she was sinking. She grabbed at the slush and at some small icicles but nothing held. Like fairy dust, whatever she touched broke and dissipated. Her hand searched up and down, front and back. It was happening too fast. With her ice ax she tried to self-arrest. There was nothing to hit it into, nothing to hold on to. Bits of snow and ice struck her in the face, in her eyes, sharp pieces sticking out of her hair–like chignon pins. She tried to scream and got a mouthful of snow. Time stood still and what took a second to occur seemed to her to last an hour. Every detail of her slide loomed large in her mind as if they were the last moments of her life. There was nothing to do. She tried to pray and found that she couldn't. She knew what happened when you slid unroped into a glacial crevasse. There was only one outcome.

Slipping along the underground wall of ice, she felt the cold, smooth slickness against her and wondered how much longer she would continue downward. Her courage gone, she closed her eyes.

There were shouts. She heard her name. It sounded far off, as in a dream. Something rough and wiry was brushing against her face. Slowly she opened her eyes. The blackness was total. She felt safer with her eyes closed again.

The shouts came louder. "Dana, Dana," Gary was calling. Through the haze of snow, slush, and ice, blackness and confusion, the urgency of his sound broke through. "Grab the rope, grab the rope, grab the rope, Dana! Grab the rope!"

That thing against her cheek, it was the rope, she thought dazedly. Tentatively she tried to lift her arm. It seemed to take so long to move anything. And then suddenly a great joy filled her as she realized she wasn't falling anymore. She was alive. She felt her hand clutch against the steely braid. They were going to pull her up! She gave a small yank in signal. The rope was drawn up. She tried to hold on. Inexplicably, it slid through her grasp. Once again she was clawing at air. Her breath came in small gasps. She was suffocating. She knew it. It was no use. How far down she was she could not tell. The next moments were of silence, of fear so tangible and consuming she thought it would make an indelible imprint upon this great glacier.

"I'm coming, babe. I'm coming. Hold on. Just a little longer." For what seemed like an eternity but was probably more like five minutes, Dana waited. Finally Gary was beside her, having belayed into the crevasse. Throwing her over his shoulder in a fireman's hold, he signaled for Bill and Joe to tow them up. Her head spinning, she could not sort out what was happening. It was only when she was stretched out on the pulverized glacial rock, her head resting on a pack, her eyes focusing with difficulty on the illuminated sky and on Gary's anxious face, that she knew the miracle of her rescue.

"Dana, Dana, Dana," Gary whispered her name over and over. Cradling her face between his palms, he bent over her. She thought she saw a small glimmer of unshed tears in the corners of his eyes. But then she thought that no, it must have been her imagination, or the play of starlight and snow. "Are you hurt?" he asked gently.

Trying to raise herself, Dana sank back on the nylon headrest. "Just winded. Nothing's broken, except maybe my spirit," she added as an afterthought. She gave a little laugh. She felt Gary moving her legs and arms to ascertain for himself just how "winded" she was.

"The only casualty was your pack," he announced in a relieved voice after his skilled examination.

"Oh, no!" Dana exclaimed, feeling behind her with one hand. "How did that happen?"

"The ice must have sheared it off," Gary answered with the only plausible response. "Lucky you didn't have too much in it."

"I had my sleeping bag!" she pouted. "This is a nice fix! What am I going to do without my sleeping bag?"

"There are extra sleeping bags at Camp Three. If our luck holds out, those clouds that just formed over there won't turn into a blizzard on us and we'll make it to Three. Are you up to climbing, Dana?"

"Nothing could hold me back," she said firmly, despite her shakiness.

Joe looked chastened, as if he felt guilt for having been miffed at Dana. "I'm glad you're safe and unharmed. Those crevasses can be sneaky."

Gary looked searchingly at Dana. "Don't be a martyr. If you feel unnerved, nobody will blame you. Another day at camp might help us all acclimate better to the altitude."

His kindness was not lost upon her though she nonetheless felt humiliated. She told herself what was the truth, that anybody in the lead most likely would have fallen in the crevasse.

"Let's rope up this time and get going before those clouds do develop into something." She tried to draw attention away from herself. "The weather is so unpredictable here."

As they were nearing the end of the glacier the actual climbing lay just ahead. That and the rope around her brightened Dana's spirits. Pitons, ice screws, carabiners, and some ropes had been left in place on previous days so the interminable waiting that was part of mountaineering was missing on this leg of the climb. They watched for loose rock and ice, but for the most part they climbed steadily upward, levering themselves, emerging on the face and working their way with ropes from one already-known hand- and foothold to the next.

After some hours of vertical climbing they reached a deep gully that cut through the face of the rock. It was not difficult to cross, since it was diagonal and presented no special problems. There were no ice spires overhead, no overhangs to negotiate; they could walk rather than climb. This they did and for the first time since the latter part of their glacial trek they walked together rather than using ropes.

That easy break did not last long, however, and in fifteen minutes they were roping up again. Dana loved watching Gary climb; he always looked as if he were moving without effort, without thought. He never hesitated, never took a false step. Dana admired his concentration. He seemed totally oblivious to the occasional shower of pebbles and ice that rained down on his face. Joe and Bill were also, Dana could see, quite competent climbers and Dana, despite her mishap, felt pride and confidence in the team.

"Off belay," Gary shouted, breaking into Dana's reveries and forcing her to take her eyes off his powerful form clinging to the rock and ice above her.

Securing the rope around her, Dana called out, "Climbing." It took her an exhilarating few minutes to reach Gary. It was a time where all uncertainty, all fear, was gone, a time of single-minded pursuit. It was a time when the consciousness of Gary's presence left her. Her mind was filled with handholds and angles at which to place her toes.

Immediately as she stood beside him, the single-minded focus of her climbing melted and she felt as if someone had put another slide into the projector that was her mind. She was full of thoughts of him once more. She ached to put out her hand against the bulging muscles of his arms, to pull down the zipper of his parka just enough for her to reach in her hand and lay it against his chest. She wanted to press her lips against the palm of his hand and let him know that he was the best, the most perfect of men.

The air must be making her light-headed, she thought,

as the perfidy of her own thoughts struck her. She was being unfaithful to the mountain.

"Your forefinger is white," Gary commented. "Looks like a seizure of the capillary. Why don't you suck it?"

"It will be all right." Dana brushed aside his suggestion. "That often happens to me."

Impatiently grabbing her hand, Gary put his lips around her finger. "First aid," he explained, holding her freezing finger in his hand momentarily. The sucking, drawing motions of his mouth on her finger did more to her than restore circulation. His eyes glinted piercingly under the arctic sky. Her eyes were opened wide. Her trembling, she knew, was not due to the cold.

Lowering her eyes, she pulled her finger from him. "As good as new," she said lightly. "Thanks for the therapy."

"I'm good at all sorts of therapy," he bantered, "especially physical."

"You're an incorrigible flirt," she laughed, relieved that he had distanced himself from her with his words, "but I do believe that underneath that warm, funny exterior is a heart of ice."

"Wrong," he pronounced. "I'm just a big wild outdoorsman waiting to be domesticated."

"I doubt that," she answered more seriously. "You're too autonomous. You don't need anybody except yourself and maybe the mountains. You open yourself to people only so far. I know. I've been observing you."

He replied with a hearty laugh. "I'm flattered that you've found me interesting enough to observe, what with all this natural beauty around. But I have to tell you one thing. Your powers of observation leave something to be desired."

Their conversation was cut short by Joe who'd just

128

joined them, out of breath and faintly green. "Altitude sickness," he panted. "I must be getting old."

"At the ripe old age of twenty-four, I'd say you've got a couple of good years left in you, Joe," Dana kidded him.

"You going to be able to make it, Flynn?" Gary asked quietly.

"Yeah, no problem. This has happened before and it'll happen again. I look worse than I feel."

Gary nodded and the three of them waited silently until Bill reached them. For the next several hundred feet the climbing was easy. Although they were roped up, Dana felt that it almost wasn't necessary, unless, of course, you happened to look down. Then it could get slippery, more a result of nerves than steep incline. The panorama was incredible. For miles and miles she could see snowy peaks, mountain ranges, glaciers, valleys, and rivers of ice. There was a different kind of air, a different kind of light in the mountain. With each step her exultation grew, until, at times, she felt she could no longer contain her joy and would break out in a spontaneous laugh or smile.

Almost as if to compensate for the ease of the past few hundred feet, they came to an incredibly difficult piece of climbing. It was just past the second camp at which they had decided to make only a pit stop. Dawn had broken and they had only a few hours of safe climbing in which to make the third camp. What faced them now was an abbreviated version of the Black Dike she had tried to climb with Gary back in New Hampshire. The icicle they faced was wider than the Dike and about seventy-five feet shorter. It was impossible to avoid, for it was surrounded on both sides by gullies over which lay thin ice bridges. Most likely the bridges would hold a climber's weight, but if it didn't, the drop would be into infinity. So it was climb the icicle or nothing. Not having accompanied Gary and Bill to Camp Three, this was Dana's first meeting with this particular icicle. She sucked in her breath and prayed that she would meet with no mishap as she had on the Dike. The icicle would take a lot of time for, due to the ever-changing conditions of ice, it had been impossible to leave in ice screws.

It was that time between night and dawn when things looked particularly eerie on the mountain. Dana's muscles hurt from the exertion of the climb, but as well as any of the men there she struggled valiantly up the steep icicle. After that ordeal they passed a wall of ice on a terrifyingly thin succession of translucent footholds. Almost at the limit of her strength, Dana longed for rest. What she had been doing the last hours easily ranked with the most difficult climbing that a mountaineer could do.

As if nature had placed an obstacle course in their way for this leg of the climb, they next had to cross a snowy gully. As they plunged into the snow they found to their horror that it was not frozen at all. Instead, it was almost like walking across a slushy marshland.

"We should have done this three weeks earlier in the season," Gary muttered darkly. He was clearly disgruntled, first with the slush on the glacier and now with this. "We're going to make it. We're going to make it."

It didn't take long for their waterproof clothing, guaranteed or your money back, to become drenched. There was no talking now in the party. They waded through the slush as quickly as possible. Hypothermia was on everybody's mind. They knew that it was only a matter of time before the fatal lowering of body temperature set in. They had to make camp and soon. If the weather held out, there would be no insurmountable problem. But ominous, dark clouds had swept in from the west.

Dana scanned the sky worriedly. In Alaska's mountains, blinding blizzards blew up with little or no warning. Thus far, they had been spared the vagaries of the weather. If they could make it to camp, they would be safe, blizzard or not.

At this point they divided into pairs. Gary and Dana were roped together, Bill and Joe together. Gary led the way. The sheer rock wall was made shiny with its coating of ice. Two relatively close ridges divided it, providing convenient places to rest and take sustenance.

"Off belay," came Gary's familiar call as he reached the higher ridge.

"Climbing," came Dana's reply.

The wind had picked up, whistling around her ears with a sound reminiscent of a dentist's high-speed drill. Just next to her the wind caused a small ice slide to rattle down the face. Her heart beat wildly as she felt the first wet snow and ice falling about and on her. The storm was building. The rope was slick with hardened ice, making it difficult to grasp. She had ten feet to go before joining Gary in safety on his ledge. Swirls of ice and snow flew around her, almost blinding her. She felt as if she were climbing alone, Gary being almost lost from view by the white flakes enveloping them both. For the second time since the beginning of the expedition she wondered if she would become another mountaineering statistic. She thought she heard Gary calling to her, but his words were muffled and lost by the wind that had grown to almost gale force in a matter of minutes, hammering at her, making her sway, reedlike. The peace she had felt on gazing at the gigantic peak of McKinley was replaced now with terror, naked and wild, as nature unleashed its fury upon her. She had to keep going. She could do it. She could hold on.

Her fingers were frozen, the cold having intensified. It was such an effort, she thought numbly, to grab hold of the rock. She moved her hand and felt herself missing the hold. Her body arched involuntarily as she began to slip.

"Tension!" she cried, knowing full well that he could not hear her over the storm.

Miraculously the rope tightened around her, catching her, and then hoisting her steadily up the frozen face. Despite the elements screaming and howling around her, she thankfully gave up the fight, trusting Gary and putting her life entirely in his hands. Her feet finally on solid ground, she looked at Gary standing next to her on the wide ledge. He seemed as shaken as she.

"I thought for a minute that you were lost," he shouted above the howling wind. "I can't remember a worse time in my life."

"Lost and found," she answered with a shiver. "Thanks."

CHAPTER EIGHT

Gary pointed at a cavelike recess in the mountain within which he had already laid his pack.

"Flynn and Lewis will ride out the storm all right down on the lower ridge. It's a wide enough shelf. As for us"—he looked at his wet, frozen, trembling companion—"we'd better warm up, or we're going to be in trouble." He motioned her toward the farthest wall of the shallow cave.

Unrolling his sleeping bag, Gary lay two chocolate bars on the head roll.

"Get out of those wet clothes before they harden and we have to hammer them off," he said lightly, trying to take the edge off a tense situation.

"You go into the sleeping bag first," she stammered. "I won't freeze to death, don't worry."

"We're not taking turns," he said with no-nonsense authority.

"You expect me to share your one-man sleeping bag?" she asked nonplussed.

133

"Yes."

"And you want me to take my clothes off? And you're going to take your clothes off too?" she continued in a tone that suggested that he ought to be committed. Despite the tone, she knew it was taking her too long to form the words. Her teeth were chattering hard and her thought processes seemed slowed.

"I realize," he said with a flash of amusement, "that propriety, nay, chastity ranks high on your list of priorities, but I somehow assumed that life ranked higher. Of course, if you'd rather die of hypothermia than lie naked next to me, I'm sure even though you're not a member, that there would be many eulogies written in your behalf by the Society of American Virgins. Not," he quickly amended the insinuation inherent in his words, "that there would necessarily be anything unchaste about raising one's body temperature a point or two."

"You just saved my life," she said, as if just realizing it.

"Ah." He shrugged with stiff palms upturned. "I was just hanging around anchored to a piton with nothing to do, so I figured, what the hell, I might as well save a life today," and then more sternly he added, "If you don't strip and get into that sleeping bag, it will have been a lot of wasted effort."

"So you saved my body and you're damning my soul!" she laughed ironically.

Gary grimaced. "No, I'm saving your body and soul."

"Is that a threat?" How she managed to be coy when she was shaking so, she could not fathom.

"Only if you want it to be." As he spoke, Gary fished out a bottle of sherry from which he poured two generous cupfuls.

"Drink this," he ordered her, downing the libation in one gulp.

The liquid burned her throat as she followed his example, creating a welcome warmth in her stomach that contrasted with the icy condition of the rest of her body and which also made her realize that Gary was right. His lips were blue. She had no doubt that hers were also. Despite the sherry she could not stop shivering. A feeling of sleepiness was threatening to overcome her. That was a sign of impending hypothermia which, although it could simply mean that she was tired, could not be ignored. To enter a sleep from which she would not awaken was not something she intended to do for at least a half century. Her inner voice and Gary's stern voice spoke clearly to her of danger.

"You'll have to turn around," she slurred, the words being difficult to form. Her tongue was feeling heavy and too big for her mouth.

Gary nodded, rather too fast and too many times, she thought through a mind that was becoming alarmingly sluggish. He, too, was losing control, she realized. Time was running out. So why, she thought dimly, was she concerned with modesty?

Watching his back, she unzipped her parka, pulled off her crampons, her boots, her socks. Her feet were stark white, she thought, no different in color than the snow. She had to hurry. The buttons on the neck of her wool sweater kept slipping out of her grasp. It took four tries to successfully complete the operation. Finally, when she pulled her sweater over her head, tore off her cotton jersey, and came to her thermal underwear, she realized with a sinking feeling that she had hoped that they were still dry, despite the sticking feeling against her skin. They were not

135

quite as soaked as the outer layers of clothing, but they were decidedly moist. As quickly as she could, which again turned out to be not very quickly at all, she stepped out of her underwear, removed her bra and panties, and feeling that if she waited one more half second she would die of the cold, she jumped into Gary's sleeping bag, huddling against one side with her knees drawn up to her chest. Her teeth were chattering so hard she feared she would bite through her tongue. Squeezing her eyes shut, she willed herself to relax and thought that her shaking and shivering was a good sign. It meant that her body was still working to warn her against the cold, that she had not passed the point of no return.

Peeling his clothes with alacrity, Gary was beside her, similarly positioned toward the opposite side of the sleeping bag in what seemed barely a matter of seconds. Despite the conditions, Dana felt herself blushing as their buttocks brushed against each other. Tentatively straightening her legs out so that she could press her entire length against the side of the sleeping bag, thereby avoiding contact with Gary, she found that her shivering, rather than abating, increased, making her involuntarily draw up her legs again. Beside her she could sense Gary shaking with cold.

"Y-y-you'd b-b-better t-turn ar-r-round," he said through teeth that chattered as badly as her own.

"I-I-I d-d-don't think so," she replied.

"T-t-turn around!" he ordered sharply. "B-believe m-me, sex is the l-last thing on m-my mind. Even you, my ice princess, c-couldn't t-turn me on in this c-condition. Now!" he said sternly but with a hint of humor, "I hope you're r-r-ready to f-follow orders."

Reluctantly she turned to him. Unaccountably a lump rose in her throat as she remembered that other time she had lain with him, that awful, humiliating time in Boston. She closed her eyes against the memory.

"I know this isn't easy for you, after what happened in your apartment," he said, uncannily perceptive, "but try to think of it as first aid for both of us. I'm sorry about Boston."

She felt him shivering against her. His hands, as they encircled her, were as cold as the ice sculpture he had carved back at base camp. Again her teeth began chattering so uncontrollably that she could not say anything. He pressed against her. She became aware of the goose bumps standing out on her arms and shoulders. Despite the cold, the wind, and the snow that still swirled around the entrance of their small cave, Dana was exquisitely conscious of his skin, hairy and coarse in places, silken in others, rubbing against her. She felt the power and strength of his body, and even knowing the precariousness of their situation she felt momentarily safe. Safe, that is, until embarrassment washed over her to become her overriding emotion. She felt a warm flush and a cold shudder throughout her whole body. Her nipples were hard and pointy from the cold, and she could feel them poking through the hairy layer that covered his broad chest.

Gary reached his hand over his head toward the Hershey bars and peanuts he had negligently dropped on the head roll earlier. Somehow they had dropped behind and perhaps propelled by a gust of wind had landed several feet beyond his grasp.

"We're not going to make it this way. Our furnaces are low," Gary said in an unnatural voice. "We've got to get that candy and nuts, and I wouldn't recommend that one of us get out and walk over. Help me on this, will you,

Dana. We've got to move in unison to get us and our temporary home over to the fuel lines."

As they squirmed their way over to the nuts and chocolate, her breasts bouncing against his chest, stomachs straining, hips and thighs tangling, they not only created enough friction against the floor of the cave in order to locomote but managed to warm up somewhat in the process. Unzipping the top of the sleeping bag just enough to wriggle out about a foot, Gary managed to retrieve the nuts and candy but not before a draft of arctic air chilled both of them to the bone once more.

Greedily tearing open the waterproof packages, they ate. The chocolate indeed provided instant energy and the nuts protein, which would burn more slowly. As a modicum of comfort returned, so did her embarrassment. Lying nude with a man in a sleeping bag, chomping on chocolate and nuts, halfway up an Alaskan mountain was not the proper way for a woman of her upbringing to behave. Especially given the somewhat peculiar relationship that existed between them. She tried as best she could to move away from Gary, not an easy maneuver in a one-man sleeping bag. In the process of rolling on her side, her thigh grazed against him.

Trying to normalize the situation and ease her own discomfort, Dana asked, "Since we're on close enough terms to share a sleeping bag, I'm curious about something."

"Shoot," Gary replied, his mouth full of peanuts.

"What's the story about that environmental case down in Fairbanks? That is, if it's not too personal."

Gary laughed heartily. The color seemed to have returned to his lips.

"As I told you, the issue of protecting the land is impor-

138

tant to me. And certain legal aspects of the case interest me. I went to law school."

"You did?" she asked, astonished. "What happened, did you flunk out?"

He laughed. "On the contrary, I was a straight A student and moot-court winner. I realized, though, I didn't want to make a lot of money as a hired gun for the corporations."

"Is that it? You just don't like to make money? Does it make you feel guilty?"

"No, that's not it at all. I come from a long line of attorneys, all of whom were very rich, very successful, and very bright. Yet, their contributions to society, to culture, or to their own fulfillment amounted to zero. Like lots of lawyers, and I guess others, too, they were the best and the brightest and they sold out for the bucks. I didn't want to be one of them."

Dana didn't know what to say, since his sentiments mirrored hers so precisely, yet she doubted that he would believe her if she told him. Deciding against it, she asked again about the environment case.

"It involves rezoning, so to speak, a vast tract of federally protected land. The details aren't important right now. Just let's say I'm on the side of the good guys."

Dana's small laugh was soundless. How admirable he was, how much like herself he sounded.

Misinterpreting her reaction, Gary recoiled from her as much as their tight quarters allowed.

"I suppose I sound ridiculous to you. You're probably thinking that I'm a pompous self-righteous ass."

"Not at all," she hastened to say. "I respect you for it."

It was Gary's turn to laugh, albeit humorlessly. "Sweet. You're a supporter of the first amendment and you learned that everyone is guaranteed freedom of speech. So you respect my right to hold any job I want. Thank you. I'm glad you're a liberal."

The unjustified rebuke stung her sharply. "I suppose," he continued, "that to confide such sentiments to a collector of Lladro and a patron of designer salons is asking for trouble. I shouldn't have expected your sympathy. I don't need it. Nobody has to say, 'Hey, Gary, you're great! You're a hero!' What do I want from you anyway? You are who you are."

Dana felt her newly returned color draining from her face. Damn him! And damn that Lladro! What did he want from her? And why was he doing this? He was as changeable as a chameleon, and she didn't know what to make of it. One minute he was saving her life, the next he was solicitous and sweet and funny. Then he was, though he said nothing, aroused. Finally he patronized her, cut her to the quick with harsh words and a lack of understanding.

"What you seem quite accomplished at is jumping to conclusions. Maybe if you had stayed in law school you wouldn't have had to go around borrowing money from women you hardly know." Dana gulped as she finished her sentence. She hadn't meant to say that, Dana thought frantically. Why had she?

Gary fairly bristled with rage. The thought that the amount of static electricity in the air between them at that moment was enough to electrocute somebody crossed Dana's mind.

"You'll get your money back. As soon as we get off this mountain. It will be the first thing I do." He frowned severely; the hint of wariness she had seen in his eyes was replaced now with cold disdain.

Each turned sideways toward opposite ends of the sleeping bag, shuddering with what Dana could interpret only as revulsion when their legs or backs involuntarily touched.

Dana shook her head. She was completely puzzled at the turn their conversation had taken. It had started out amicably enough. Now it seemed that they were the worst of enemies. It had been his fault, hadn't it? No, she answered herself. She had caused it with her perversity. Why couldn't she tell him how wrong he was about her? She expected him to be clairvoyant. No man could know what was in a woman's mind, not unless she told him, or showed him. She did neither, telling and showing the opposite of what she felt to be true. Why? she wondered. Was it vulnerability she was afraid of? If she heard him say, Take a walk, lady, to the woman she really was, how much more hurtful that would be than to hear those same words said to the woman she was not.

"I hate Lladro," she heard herself say aloud.

"What?"

"I hate Lladro," she insisted once again. To the sound of his chuckles she added, "My mother sends it to me, and I don't care about the ten thousand dollars. I don't want it back. Donate it to your favorite charity."

"You'll get it and *you* donate it to *your* favorite charity." He softened, and took her hair in his hands, for he had positioned himself facing her again. "You, my dear, are a study in contradictions. You hate Lladro, yet it's all over your apartment. You don't care about the money, yet you bring it up every chance you get."

"I suppose," she answered in a small voice, "it's because I'm so used to rebelling I do it without thinking. You know, I never met anyone like you before. You don't fit nicely into any of my categories."

"Neither do you into any of mine," he replied softly. "I know you were a spoiled little rich girl who's grown into a spoiled, rich woman. And I know you're good at hiding it. You've learned, no doubt, that people don't take kindly to grown-up princesses. Despite that"—he stroked her hair gently—"I like you. I like you very much. I also like that you have the sensitivity to know you ought to be rebelling even if you haven't got it all straight in your mind. One day," he said wistfully, "when you're where you want to be, I hope you'll look me up."

Still, he didn't think her worthy of him. Still, he condescended to her, she thought unhappily. "Maybe I will look you up one day," she answered briskly, "that is, if we ever get off this mountain." On a more practical note, he added, "Our clothes are soaked and they'll never dry in the heap we've left them."

"You're right," he grinned. "Should we wriggle over together?"

"Why doesn't one of us go and the other can keep the sleeping bag warm? We can toss for it," she suggested.

"I'll go." He scampered to his feet and ran with his toes barely touching the ground before they were lifted in another step. With lightning speed he managed to pull out two pitons and a rope from his pack, which he fashioned into a makeshift clothes line. Tying the wet garments to the line, they immediately began dancing in the wind that blew through the cave.

Dana knew she shouldn't be following his progress with her eyes, but she couldn't tear her gaze from his beautifully muscled body. His buttocks were smooth, and firm. She yearned to feel him against her. Quickly she banished the

142

thought. Anyway, she would be feeling him against her, icy cold. Only by warming him with her own body would she be able to stave off the painful effects of exposure for him.

"*Aiiiieeeee,*" he yelped in a high-pitched tone as he jumped back into the sleeping bag. "F-f-freezing out there!"

"If I ever get married," she intoned calmly, "it will *not* be to a man with cold feet!" Catching his icy toes between her calves, she pressed gently.

"H-h-how can you make j-j-jokes at a time like th-this?" he stammered.

Placing Gary's hands under her armpits to warm them, she answered soothingly, "In an insane situation it's the only way to keep hold of my sanity."

"I-if I had any sensation in my hands, I m-m-might be enjoying myself," he retorted.

"Not me. Having ice cubes thrust into my armpits is not my idea of fun," Dana said, trying to distance herself from the bizarre situation and from her awareness of his cold wrists against the sides of her breasts. Despite Gary's pain and despite the fact that this was accepted procedure, Dana worried that Gary would interpret her action as immodest and forward. His inscrutable look with what she thought was just a hint of a smile was no comfort to her.

"The blizzard's getting worse," Gary said kindly, sensing her embarrassment. "Looks like it's going to be a big one."

Dana looked toward what appeared to be an opaque white curtain just outside their alcove. Visibility was zero. "We're lucky we ended up here," Dana observed. "I hope Bill and Joe are making out okay."

143

"Don't worry. They may not be quite as protected as we are, but don't forget, they've got two sleeping bags. They're not suffering the same hardship that I am. Being forced to share your sleeping bag with a luscious, naked woman deserves combat pay."

"Maybe so, but it certainly doesn't deserve having your own living handwarmer," Dana said, abruptly removing his hands from their warm abode.

"Me and my big mouth," Gary said abjectly.

"Perhaps you'd do better by both of us if you stuck your cold hands in your big mouth," Dana retorted.

The silence that followed had a soothing quality as they watched the snowfall from their snug little hideaway, something like the lulling effect of watching flames leap about in a fireplace. Despite the situation, his remarks, and their past, her skin hungered for his touch. "Have you ever been stuck in a blizzard before?" Dana asked.

"Yes." He drew out the word thoughtfully. "But not quite in these circumstances. Once with my brother, when he still liked to climb before he became so involved in his law career, we were stuck for three days in the Swiss Alps. Neither of us knew much about climbing in those days, so we decided to stick it out until the weather cleared completely. We must have had a month's worth of food with us," Gary chuckled fondly.

"Do you see much of your brother?" she asked.

"Not as much as I'd like. My family's down in Connecticut now. When we get together it's usually for holiday dinners. My family has always been susceptible to workaholism, and my brother has got a particularly bad case of it."

"But you don't have that same susceptibility?" she inquired.

"No, I could have had it, but then I realized that my life was passing me by and I didn't know what I was studying torts for. Except financially, the practice of law would have been very unrewarding for me. Now that I've got myself a little store, I do all the climbing and dreaming and reading I want. I'm a free man."

"I would hardly call your store little," she interjected.

"All right, my little big store then," he chuckled, and he stretched out as far as he could.

"That's interesting," Dana remarked lamely.

"Did you think I was some sort of mountain bum when I showed up at your parents' house in Scarsdale?"

"No," she lied, laughing, "but now I think you're a mountain goat!"

"R-r-r-roar," he bellowed. "I'll show you what kind of a goat I am—a satyr, a horned goat!" Playfully he lunged for her neck, which he nuzzled with his two-day growth of beard.

"Cut it out!" Laughingly she pushed him away. She sobered as she thought that they were cavorting as if they were fully dressed, or as if they were innocent children. Neither was true. "Bill and Joe might hear and think you're trying to reach them."

"Women are all the same. Quiet, the neighbors will hear," Gary mocked her.

"We've been up since two this morning. We should probably nap a little so we're refreshed," Dana said reasonably in an attempt to establish a more businesslike atmosphere. She hadn't, after all, chosen to take off her clothes. It had been literally a do-or-die situation. "What time is it anyway?"

He turned to stare at her and said simply, "It's time." Though his unshaven face was shadowed and his black hair matted, the handsome strength of his visage stunned Dana. His steady gaze and peremptory tone left no doubt as to his meaning.

Dana met his gaze as they lay on their sides facing each other. She felt his hand on her uplifted hip, slowly, tantalizingly, outlining its form and then gently pushing it down. He continued to trace her hip, extending his touch down her outer thigh. Dana was hit by the freshness of the sensations caused by Gary's gentle, yet inexorable caresses. She realized he was in no hurry as he lingered over her hip even as his lips sought hers. Dana felt safe, bound even, in their little sleeping bag.

Finally his muscled torso stretched along hers with what she thought was a shiver of anticipation. It certainly could not be due to the cold, since the temperature both physically and emotionally was quite warm. Sensing Gary's determination to move slowly, Dana lay languidly back as she answered Gary, kiss for interminable kiss, movement for thrilling movement.

"Oh, Dana, I've wanted you for a long time."

Her taut nipples were like rosy pearls buried in the fine hairs of his broad chest as she responded. "And I've wanted you, too, Gary."

His deliberateness was sweet torture as his hands roamed plunderingly over her soft flesh, always returning to each spot over and over. He worshipped her body with his hands, his lips, and his own body. Dana, despite the cold outside, felt as if she were a flower blossoming in a hothouse. She lost herself in a warm haze of sensation, slowly ebbing and rebuilding again. Gary's strong back and stomach, his thighs and the hard muscles of his buttocks honed by the rigors of climbing, were thrilling to touch as the boundary between them seemed to melt in the haze of their lovemaking.

With the snow falling steadily and their complete isolation, time seemed to truly have stopped. All that existed for Dana was Gary, whose strength and intensity filled her with desire, whose hands and lips caressed her body incessantly, now fast, now gently, now demanding. "Gary, oh, Gary . . ."

"My sweet lady." Gary kissed her mouth closed. Dana could only sigh as his lips lightly kissed her neck and collarbone. His hands caressed her breasts as he lowered his head to her nipples and gently licked them. Her body arched languidly as his strong arm under her lower back pulled her to him.

When her sensations had built to such an exquisite peak that they were almost unbearable, Gary entered her slowly, yet relentlessly. Dana's arms and legs enveloped him, her hips surged up to meet his as they continued their lovemaking, finding their own ethereal rhythm. Their supple bodies rocking in unison, Dana opened to him completely as she swam in a warm sea of love. She gasped as a tidal wave of sensation rolled over her. Her movements were involuntary, as if some elemental aspect of her had been awakened by Gary's maleness and was responding to it on its own. Gary's hair, skin, scent, hardness, filled her senses. She burst with pleasure as his body shuddered. They clung to each other as cascades of pleasure broke over them.

Finally they were immobile. They lay together, serene and languid. "Talk about the thrills of mountain climbing," Gary kidded lightly. "Dana, I . . ."

Dana covered his mouth with her hand and rested her head on his chest. The sound of his strong heart added to

147

her contentment. The natural feeling of coziness engendered by being warm when it was cold outside was multiplied a thousand times. Dana was safe and warm and happy.

The altitude, the isolation, and the snow all conspired to create an eerie feeling of timelessness, as if they were butterflies waiting in their own little cocoon. Gary's easy caressing once again began to quicken, and Dana felt her barely rested passions beginning to stir once more. With the empty hours before them and the languor induced by their lovemaking and the elevation, they proceeded at a sensuously slow pace. Gary's hands wandered over Dana's body as they embraced in a miasma of unhurried pleasure. His strong fingers gripped her thighs and explored the silken recess between them. Dana didn't try to think but let herself become open to all sensation. Even the nylon lining of the sleeping bag felt like satin to her. She kissed his chest, loving the prickly feel of his curls against her lips. She closed her mouth upon the hard knot of his muscular arm and marveled at his perfect maleness.

When he entered her again, Gary undulated slowly, inexorably. Establishing once again their own personal rhythm, they loved away the day, oblivious to their snowy surroundings. The whistling wind, their pounding hearts, the rustling of their bodies, were celestial music to their ears. Hours later, Dana confessed, "I'm worried."

"Why?"

"You've heard about the earth moving at times like this?"

"Yes, and . . . ?" Gary obligingly responded.

"Well, here it would lead to an avalanche." Dana giggled.

Spent and exhausted, they slept.

"Climbing!" Bill's voice reverberated through the crystalline mountain air.

"Looks like our sweet interlude is over, my darlin'. We'd better get dressed," Gary said. Unzipping the sleeping bag enough to permit him to wriggle out, he ran over to the makeshift clothesline he had fashioned. Watching him, Dana thought worriedly that usually when she heard the word *interlude,* it was used with adjectives like *brief* or *meaningless.* Hurrying back, Gary stuffed Dana's ice-cold but mountain-air-dried garments into the sleeping bag, and climbed in with his clothes.

"Cold enough for you?" Dana joshed. The spring temperature on McKinley averaged twenty-five degrees below zero, and the winter temperature at one hundred below was the coldest recorded on earth.

"No, it's balmy, all the way up to fifteen below zero," Gary responded, shivering. "Will you warm up my hands?" His mouth crooked in an irresistible boyish grin.

"Again," she answered coyly. "All right."

"But I've got a better place," he whispered as he thrust his cold hands against the silken warmth of her inner thighs. The chill of his hands fanned the flame that was still smoldering inside her.

"They're going to be here soon," she said regretfully after a few minutes.

Gary nodded as they both made use of all their acrobatic skills to dress themselves in the warmth of the sleeping bag. Though Gary once put his leg in her long underwear, they managed to get dressed enough to get out of the bag in order to don their outerwear and footgear before Bill and Joe arrived.

"Hey, guys!" Joe's head peeked over the edge of ice and rock.

"Joe!" Gary's voice boomed unnaturally loud. "How did you make out?"

Busy clipping the rope to a carabiner so that Bill could climb up, Joe took his time in answering. "Off belay," he shouted down.

"Climbing," came the traditional response.

Over his shoulder Joe filled them in. "We decided when the storm hit that we'd be able to make it down thirty feet to a protected overhang almost as luxurious as this one."

Within a few minutes Bill had joined them. They sat around in a circle drinking instant coffee. Dana was all too aware of the unrolled sleeping bag off to the side and of the unspoken questions.

"I take it you two weathered the storm without mishap," Bill asked quietly. "Passed the time all right?"

Dana could not miss the leer on Joe's face at his friend's remark, and she could guess the topic of conversation that had most amused them during the blizzard. Her irritation mounted along with her embarrassment. After all, they were right in their conjectures.

"We did what we had to," Gary answered shortly. An amused twinkle lit up his eyes. "Dana is great at twenty questions. How about you two? What did you do, a lot of reminiscing?"

"Fantasizing," Joe answered high-spiritedly. "We fantasized a lot, didn't we Bill?" He nudged his friend. "Yeah, what fantasies!" He sighed longingly.

The hairs at the back of Dana's neck prickled. She felt like slapping Joe's face, and Bill's and even Gary's. She felt as if some sort of code was being spoken by the three of them and the subject was her. It was a mistake having come up here with three men. It was a mistake having fallen in love.

"That was some blizzard," Gary remarked. "It's unusual for a storm to last so long this time of year." He shook his head. "We were lucky."

"Some of us were luckier than others," Joe cracked.

Gary's face tightened ominously. Thunderclouds seemed to amass in his eyes. His stony glare killed the laughter as it gurgled in Joe's throat.

"I, uh," Joe sputtered. "I think I'll have more coffee."

"What do you think," Bill asked quickly in an attempt to cover his friend's gaffe, "will we reach Camp Three by mid-morning?"

"I would say that's an accurate estimate. That is, if we don't spend the rest of the night drinking coffee. We'll break for the day at camp and start out for the summit around two A.M."

After guzzling the remainder of their coffee, forcing themselves to drink two glasses of water in order to avoid dehydration, and snacking on dried fruit, biscuits, and honey, they set out for the long night's trek to the final camp before their bid for the summit.

CHAPTER NINE

Relieved to be in camp at last and in possession of her own sleeping bag, no sooner had she stretched out than Dana was sound asleep. The climb, the altitude, not to mention the manner in which she and Gary had passed the previous day, had left her exhausted. The thin, dry air made breathing difficult and Dana noted with some consternation that she had experienced a fleeting sensation of dizziness. Joe, Bill, and even Gary all seemed to be very fatigued. At least Dana hoped it was fatigue, which explained why Gary had, since leaving, treated her with all the warmth a distracted cashier reserves for customers. On the other hand, she appreciated his seeming disinterest because of the snide remarks Bill and Joe had made. It might make them think there actually was nothing of a romantic nature between the two of them. She was confused, whether by Gary or the altitude, she didn't know. She drifted off to sleep thinking of Gary sleeping in what she momentarily imagined to be their bed.

Eight hours later, after what felt like twenty minutes sleep, they awoke at two A.M. "Boy, what I'd give for some pancakes and sausages right now," Joe remarked all too cheerily.

"Yeah, let's send out for some. What street are we on," Bill continued the jocularity.

"McKinley Drive, seventeen thousand feet up. Tell them to hold the sausages and bring extra syrup," Gary chimed in.

Dana's smile was strained. This ol'-boy joshing made her feel left out. She had never been very good in groups. She felt jealous of the others' easy camaraderie. It was this feeling of apartness, of being different, that had plagued her throughout her life. Except that back in Scarsdale, or even in Boston, she welcomed it—or told herself that she did.

With the exception of ne'er-do-wells, most of the people she knew were concerned mostly with clothes, cars, large houses, and any other sign of material wealth that was currently in vogue. Even more than that, what made her different, she had always felt, was her lack of competitiveness. Even as a child she thought the my-daddy-is-stronger-than-your-daddy games silly. She never felt in any respect that she was better than anyone else. Nonetheless, she often felt the outsider. It was a feeling she wasn't particularly fond of. She was the kid who was always chosen last in team games and she never understood why. She was a fast runner, good at sports, and told by grown-ups that she was pretty. Yet she was also the one, when the class had an odd number of students, who had to pair up with the teacher on class trips. Perhaps, she mused, that was one reason she liked mountain climbing. It was basically a solitary sport. You were competing against no one, only the mountain. It was because she had wanted so badly to climb McKinley that she had applied for the team, though she knew that it would be comprised of more than two people. Dana had always been better one on one.

Ironically, she knew people thought her a snob. The whispers hadn't been soft enough for her to miss. Perhaps because it was common for others to misperceive her and disapprove, she kept her real self hidden, she ruminated. She had even kept that self hidden from her husband, the man who wanted a wife who traded veal Cordon Bleu recipes and who smiled like Donna Reed. That marriage had left her more wrapped up in herself than before. It had been three long years, but Gary was the first man since the divorce to chip away at part of her icy shell. But even he, or especially he, she thought with a pang, didn't know the real Dana Manchester. To him she was a spoiled rich girl with nothing better to do than seek adventure and shop for designer outfits. He didn't know that she had never been attracted to that world. Maybe, she thought, suddenly dissatisfied with the way she had been handling things, he had a point. It was a rather futile expression of independence to bang away at a typewriter trying to make ends meet when she knew that if things really got tight, she had a fat trust fund waiting to be plucked. It was a trust fund that could do a lot of good somewhere instead of making a bunch of fat bankers fatter. The seed of an idea germinated in her mind.

Now the time had come to make their final assault on the summit. Speed was of the essence. At high altitudes the sun melts ice and snow rapidly, and rocks, ice, and snow sometimes of incredible size break loose and fall. They had to make the summit by noon. Ten hours of strenuous climbing lay ahead. Since dehydration was a common problem the higher the elevation, their packs were loaded with sweet juices and Gatorade.

It was a dry, clear night with an eerie, full white moon making the surrounding glaciers and peaks glow iridescently. As they broke camp and set out, they were silent, for it soon became apparent that this last leg would surely test their stamina, skill, and courage. The route they had chosen back in Boston was a new one and as their eyes scanned it now, their hearts sank. There were no faults or knobs in the ice to provide holds, but only fine, hair-thin fissures. Every hold had to be wrest manually from the ice, and, as the leader, Gary had to do most of the work. Although there were other routes, it was too late for them to alter course. The only way out for them was up, almost straight up.

After several hours of rigorous climbing, Dana noted that Bill was visibly drooping. His breathing was more belabored than it should have been and he checked too carefully before reaching for even easily placed pitons. She wondered if Gary, climbing in his usual focused, yet effortless manner, would notice. A bit later Dana observed Gary's worried glance toward Bill. At the next small ridge Gary stopped and announced, "Why don't we rest here for a while. The altitude's really getting to me. I'm tired." His generosity of spirit moved her.

To conserve energy they sat or in Joe's and Gary's case leaned, drinking thirstily. "Well, Dana, how are you making out?" Gary asked.

"Just magnificently, thank you," Dana replied breezily.

"This should make all the society pages from Montauk to Westport. Don't you think?" he taunted.

How her attitude could change from admiration to irritation so quickly amazed her more than the remark annoyed her. "Just as likely as its being mentioned in law school alumni reviews in the News from Illustrious Dropouts column!"

"I hate to disillusion you two," Joe unnecessarily continued the line of thought, "but aside from a possible mention in the Sierra Club magazine or an article in one of the sporting life newsletters, no one is going to report this."

"Not unless there is a wedding announcement in *The New York Times,*" added Bill, who had recovered somewhat.

"No chance of that," Dana and Gary said almost in unison.

"At least you two agree on something," Joe observed.

The team grew quiet as the sun rose. Dana, however, was disturbed by the flipness of Gary's retort even though she had made the same remark. Why couldn't she take what she could so easily give? She felt a strange pain as she looked at his strong profile against the rising sun. He looked like the god of the mountain. Why did he persist in seeing her as he did? He glanced at her with a cool neutrality as if, she thought, she were some stranger he happened to pass on the northern face of Mount McKinley. Sometimes he seemed to her as cold as the mountains he climbed.

As they rose to continue their hacking at the ice and snow, a hacking which seemed the easier for the closer approach to the summit, Dana heard a low interchange between Bill and Joe.

"I wonder if she'll lose this sleeping bag before we get to the summit," Joe cracked.

Bill snickered. "Next climb I think I'll take my girl

along. She can't climb, but I'll carry her in my sleeping bag!"

The two men guffawed softly, but not so softly that Dana didn't hear. She looked swiftly above her. Busily chipping away at the ice, Gary was oblivious to any conversation going on down below. Dana felt hot, then cold. Visions of retribution filled her mind. She could, she thought wishfully, kick boulders down on their sniggering faces, cut their ropes, or maybe substitute laxatives for their chocolate bars! She ended up putting their pettiness out of her mind and concentrating on her climbing technique so that each move she made was smooth and flawless.

There was a great deal of waiting now as Gary found the way, touching the icy wall for cracks, rejecting, moving on, until at last, jamming himself against a crack, he would pound in a piton or ice screw. He never seemed to tire though the work was onerous. Then, like a mirage, after what seemed to be months of climbing, the summit loomed above them. It was majestic in its indifference. It was awesome, terrifying, exhilarating. It made Dana feel both humble and exalted. She was giddy with the knowledge that within an hour she would be standing on top of North America.

That the others felt the same way was confirmed by the ethereal glow on their faces and even by the thumbs-up gesture the three men exchanged. Joe, however, after a bit, felt compelled to remark that he was glad there were no golden arches at the peak.

It was important to exercise the greatest care now, even though jubilation made them all want to rush and take chances. There were numerous stories of mountaineers who had come within a few feet of their goal and in their

157

haste had fallen off the mountain. Still it was difficult for Dana to control her exultation. This, after all, was why she loved climbing. Reaching the summit was like winning a gold medal and no one had carried her up in a sleeping bag. She had made it on her own.

After another twenty minutes they were there. Gary, the first to arrive at the summit, raised his arms over his head, his fingers spread wide, a look of joy, fulfillment, and power suffusing his wet face. Dana was next to set foot on the peak. Hardly had she done so than Gary swooped her up and whirled her around. "We made it, girl! We made it!" Bill and Joe arrived a minute later and they all four whooped at the top of their voices, "We're here! We made it. YAHOO!" In the thrill of triumph they all hugged one another and Dana was so swept up in the emotion of the moment that she forgot her usual restraint and feeling of apartness.

The vista was breathtaking. Dana let her eyes sweep over the miles of Alaskan topography all the way to the sea. The south peak of Mount McKinley stood three hundred feet below them, a huge mass of ice pinnacles and chasms. Forbidding as it looked to them from their superior position, it was by far the easier climb. What they had achieved was not only the highest point but the most difficult as well.

They came together again, Gary hugging Dana, Dana hugging Bill, and Bill hugging Joe. In a tight circle they shouted and laughed with joy—shouts that were cut short by the small avalanche brought about by the noise and even more by the lack of oxygen four miles above sea level.

"Say cheese, everybody!" Bill whipped out his camera. "This is for posterity."

"What's this cutesy cheese business?" Gary called out.

"You deserve a well-placed snowball for that one." He lobbed a soft snowball at him.

"I've got to get you to smile, don't I? And it's got to be candid. Instead of cheese, Gary, you can say Dana."

"Or cheesecake," Joe added irreverently to the appreciative chuckles of the other two men. Refusing to let anything mar this triumph, Dana smiled amiably.

"Take one of Dana by herself," Gary addressed Bill. "I want you to send this to your mother, Dana. She'll never believe what a natural beauty you are."

"My mother knows very well what I look like," Dana answered tartly.

"Sure she does, in Cardin and Dior. She'd faint if she saw you like this!"

The thought seemed to amuse Gary while she brooded over how little Gary knew her, for she rarely wore anything but jeans at home, her parents' home included.

She stuck out her tongue for the camera.

"Is that lovely expression for me, Gary, or your mother?" Bill asked as he clicked the shutter.

"For whoever deserves it." She smiled sweetly.

After the picture sessions and celebrating, they sat for a while savoring their accomplishment and the views it afforded. Gary took out a little vial, four thimble-size glasses, and a wrapped package. "M&M's and grape juice are fine, but I think we deserve the best. We've climbed the highest, after all." He winked at Dana.

"What do you have there, Gary?" Joe asked.

"An ounce of Dom Pérignon. It's flat, but we're so high that doesn't matter." He poured each of them a thimbleful of the flat champagne. "And four chocolate eclairs."

"To an inspiring climb and a successful descent," Gary toasted. "To a taste of heaven!"

They clinked drinks, downed them in one gulp, and bit into the pastry. "And now for my next surprise," Gary said with a flourish. From his pack he withdrew four perfectly smooth, oval-shaped stones each engraved with one of their names.

Dana was touched to see DANA MANCHESTER, MT. MCKINLEY SUMMIT, APRIL 1984. "How very thoughtful of you, Gary. How sweet." Dana looked up at him, her eyes shining. Neither Joe nor Bill said anything, but she could tell that they too were pleased by Gary's gesture.

"We can leave them there in that little crevasse. The boulders and rocks will protect them," Gary said.

Dana noticed Joe huddled next to Bill. "Aw, how sweet you are, you big thoughtful hunk o' man," Joe mimicked Dana mockingly. Bill chuckled conspiratorially through his scraggly beard.

Dana glanced quickly at Gary. She could tell from the way he glowered that he, too, had overheard the exchange between the two men. When it was clear that Gary was not going to respond, Dana felt moved to do so herself. She thought better of it though. Why spoil this sublime moment of triumph by coming to blows with a pea brain such as Joe? What did irritate her though was Gary's persistent silence. She did not want a prince on a white horse saving her from fire-breathing dragons, but Gary could have at least put in a word for her climbing ability. She had, after all, pulled her own weight on this expedition, and Gary more than anybody was aware of that.

"What's next, Gary, the Matterhorn or Everest?" Bill asked amicably, having suspected that the interchange between Joe and himself had been too loudly spoken.

"Neither," Gary said thoughtfully. "I think I'll be

climbing sand dunes on a tropical island for a while. I go in for extremes."

"Going solo?" Joe asked.

Gary shrugged. "You never can tell."

Dana bit her lower lip to keep it from trembling. She felt suddenly soiled. The victory she should be celebrating with all her heart had been marred by thoughtless words or, perhaps, she mused, by an unpleasant reality. Maybe she would never have been chosen for this team had she not had a pretty face and desirable body. Maybe Gary had wanted a playmate. No, she thought, she shouldn't fall into that trap. Aside from strength, which could be compensated for in other ways, she was a better climber than either Joe or Bill.

Gary, Dana, and Joe fell into shoptalk, during which time they decided to rest on the summit until evening when they could safely start their descent. It wasn't right away, but after some time Dana noticed that Bill was unusually quiet. Occasionally he coughed, a short, hacking sound.

"You feeling up to par, Bill?" she asked with a forced lightness to her voice.

"Sure, just a little tired."

Neither Joe nor Gary noticed anything amiss. Joe had already unrolled his sleeping bag and stretched out on top of it, a beatific expression on his face. His satisfaction was unqualified. Bill sat curled up where he had dropped his pack, his knees drawn tightly up to his chest, his face ashen in color.

"Come on, Dana," Gary held out a hand to her. "Let's take a walk around up here. Let's get a good view of our kingdom. "I'm glad, Dana, that you are on my team. You're a good player."

"Would you have been as glad even if I hadn't lost my sleeping bag?" she asked flippantly.

"Now, that's unfair. You made it here on your own merits, on your own climbing merits."

"Well, then, why couldn't you make that clear to the others?" she pursued.

"As I said, you climbed to the top on your own. You can handle yourself on top too. You don't need anyone to fight your battles." He lifted her chin between his thumb and forefinger and twisted it gently toward him. "Any other merits you possess are irrelevant, except to me."

"And how are they relevant to you?" she asked recklessly.

His answer was an enigmatic half smile, and a change of subject. "Would you like to buy a house up here?" he kidded.

"Maybe a four-bedroom colonial with attached garage," Dana responded.

Gary laughed. "Listen, I want to explain something to you." Just then Bill's hacking interrupted them. "Hey, Bill, didn't I warn you to stop smoking before doing McKinley?"

"It's nothing a coughdrop won't cure," Bill answered weakly.

"Keep it down, will you. I'm trying to catch a little shut-eye here," Joe complained grumpily.

From afar Dana looked skeptically at Bill. What she saw concerned her. He was leaning over, head in his hands, an uncharacteristic pose for him. Approaching him, she touched his shoulder and asked, "Are you feeling okay? Why don't you have something to eat?"

Bill shook his head. "Nah. I don't think I could keep much down right now."

Grabbing hold of his wrist before he could object, Dana glanced at her watch and took a six-second pulse. It was racing. "Have something to drink," she said firmly. "Here. Take some of this Gatorade."

"No, I don't want anything, Dana. Thanks," he said wanly. "I'm a little tired. Let me rest." He suffered another paroxysm of coughing.

"Leave him alone. He's winded and he's got a right to be," Joe said irritably. "Women!"

"Gary!" Dana called out. "Come over here. I think this could be serious!"

"What's the matter?" he answered with the merest hint of impatience.

Running over to Gary, she whispered urgently, "I think Bill may be coming down with pulmonary edema!"

"Nah. He's been at even higher elevations. Never had a problem. Anyway, we can't move down now, in mid-afternoon."

"I don't care. His pulse is racing. He's breathing rapidly. He's nauseated and I bet if you listen to his chest you'll hear the gurgling sound that's symptomatic of pulmonary edema. If we don't get him down soon, he's liable to drown in his own body fluids. Gary"—she looked up into his eyes, his deep, piercing, warm eyes—"please, listen to me."

He looked down at her and she saw respect in his eyes and more than a little admiration.

"You know your stuff, kid. I'll listen to his chest."

Gary put his ear to Bill's chest, who, slumped over sideward, paid no attention. When he rose, Dana saw the frown creasing Gary's forehead. He didn't have to tell her what she already knew.

"Wake Joe. Tell him we're starting our descent now,"

he ordered. "Three thousand feet ought to buy him enough time. He'll come with me. Dana, you bring up the rear with Joe."

"What!" Joe whined. "You're letting a hysterical female tell you what to do now, Gary?"

"Ten minutes to get ready," Gary responded.

CHAPTER TEN

"You're a lucky man," the white-coated staff physician at Fairbanks General Hospital announced to Bill who, with tubes running out of his nose, throat, and arm, could only nod. "You'll be fine in about a week. Whichever of your three friends here saw the signs of pulmonary edema so quickly saved your life."

As he exited, the doctor smiled deferentially at the climbers, for he, as well as the entire hospital staff, knew of their accomplishment.

"Well, William," Gary addressed Bill with mock formality, "I think you have Dana to thank. Maybe you ought to buy her a drink when you get on your feet again. That is, if she's still around."

Touching his lips with his free arm, Bill blew Dana a kiss of gratitude.

There was a sound of shuffling feet behind her. It was Joe reminding Dana somewhat of a dog digging a hole. He cleared his throat. "Er, Dana, gee, uh, you know, I said some things to you and I guess about you too. Well, uh, could you kind of forget them? I'm, um, in charge of organizing an expedition to tackle Kilimanjaro next fall. It's not as challenging as McKinley, but it will be a nice change. It would be an honor to have you on the team."

Dana felt herself choking up. "I'll think about that offer. Thanks." On impulse she stood on her toes and brushed her lips against Joe's ruddy cheek.

The gratification she should have been feeling and which was rightfully hers was clouded. Why had Gary made that remark about her only possibly being around for the drink? Did he expect her to fly home now, to say good-bye to him, thank him for a good climb, and go her way? Did he think she would have made love to any man she happened to be sharing a sleeping bag with? Would he have made love to any woman? Would he have made love like that? Perhaps he thought she would even have made love to the abominable snowman had she come across him. Maybe he would have made love to a chimpanzee in order to keep warm!

"We'll let you rest now, Bill."

Gary's words cut short Dana's mulling.

Joe and Dana obediently made their farewells and left Bill with gifts of magazines and paperbacks.

"You have any plans?" Gary directed his question to Dana and Joe.

"I'm going to find me a Pac-Man game and unwind," Joe said.

"I have some things to take care of," Dana said vaguely.

"Come have lunch with me," Gary said to her.

"I'm not too hungry," she answered.

"I'll make you a light lunch at my house. Come on," he cajoled. "You've never seen my house and I'm a terrific light-lunch maker. Anyway," he winked slyly, "don't you want to see my collection of Lladro?"

"Tuna on rye is sufficient inducement," she answered. "You knew I was easy, didn't you?"

"Easy as a porcupine," he answered as they walked together to his car.

Gary's house was a spacious Swiss chalet A-frame, constructed more of windows than wood it seemed. The first floor was one large room, with a free-standing fireplace, a deep pile rug, and soft, plush sofas. The second floor consisted of two bedrooms, a study, and a luxury bathroom housing a hot tub.

"You don't seem to be leading as ascetic an existence as you pretend. The way you carry on about Scarsdale, I would have expected you to live in a one-room log cabin with a water pump and an outhouse."

"I do. This is just a friend's house I'm taking care of," Gary kidded.

"Yes, with all these photographs and memorabilia of yours all around here," Dana observed. "Looks like you were quite an athlete in high school and college."

"I was the strong silent type," Gary informed her.

"You still are."

"Are you complaining?" Gary asked with a hint of wariness in his smile.

"I don't have a right to complain, do I? Especially since I might not even be here for Bill's drink next week."

"What's that supposed to mean?" Gary asked.

"For starters, I don't know what you think of me." Dana's heart thudded. She wasn't used to opening herself up to possible rejection. Nervously she pushed her hair off of her face. Her skin, despite the protection of gel and

lotion, was rosy from sun and windburn, yet still stunningly clear.

"For starters, you're the most courageous woman I've
ever known, and a top-notch climber."

"That wasn't what I had in mind," she answered in a
strained voice.

"Well, then, what precisely did you have in mind?" His
smile was deceptively casual as he posed the question.

Squirming, Dana could well believe that he had studied
law. She felt a little bit like an environmental polluter who
was being cross-examined on the witness stand.

"You're not going to make this easy for me, are you?"
Dana asked, her exasperation mounting.

"You're quite capable of handling difficult situations.
But since you press me, I'll tell you what else I think. I
think you're beautiful. You have a beautiful, expressive
face, beautiful high cheekbones, beautiful chestnut tresses,
beautiful deep eyes, a beautiful biteable neck, beautiful
shoulders, beautiful soft arms, beautiful elbows, a sweet,
rounded little tummy, beautiful hips, beautiful, perfect
legs, beautiful kneecaps, beautiful toes, not to mention
. . ."

"Right," she broke in, "not to mention . . . How about
that light lunch you promised me?"

"One light lunch coming up," he promised. "But first
we have some business to take care of."

"I thought we took care of that the night of the blizzard," she teased with what she knew was outrageous
sauciness.

"I have a check for you." He moved to a desk drawer
from which he brought forth a certified check for ten
thousand and fifty dollars. "With interest." He explained
the fifty dollars.

Pursing her lips, thereby inadvertently accentuating the high cheekbones that Gary so admired, Dana shook her head. "I'm not a banker and I don't make my money from friends."

"Business is business," Gary answered firmly.

"You're making me angry! No, furious!" She fairly shouted. "How can you give me fifty bucks for a loan of a lousy week? Don't you think I have any principles? Not to mention pride? I don't want ten thousand and fifty dollars. I don't even want the ten thousand dollars, to tell you the truth. If you have to know . . ."

"Whoa," he tried to quiet her down, "I don't have to know anything. I'm not asking any questions!"

"I'll tell you anyway!" She heard her voice rise on a hysterical note. "I'm not keeping any of that money. I'm using it and a lot more, if you don't mind my saying so, to start a fund for ecological defense!"

Putting both his hands strongly on her shoulders, Gary stared down into Dana's face. The corners of his mouth twitched and though it seemed to her that he was trying very hard to control himself, he did not succeed. Like a dam breaking, his laughter flowed over her.

"Dana, Dana. You don't have to do that! Don't you understand? I don't want you to take your money and put it where my interests lie. If you want to spend your money on diamond bobby pins, that's fine by me. You don't have to prove yourself." His face was wreathed in smiles, as if he were an old sage scolding an adorable child.

Dana was speechless. The unmitigated gall of that man! The incredibly inflated ego! To call him conceited, vain, and blind would be to understate! After agonizing minutes, when she could almost feel her blood pressure rising, she found her voice.

"You have the temerity to think that I would actually give my money away to please you? Hah! Your head is still in the clouds, buster! Don't you think I can have interests and values of my own that have nothing to do with you? And what makes you think I would want to please you, anyway?"

An arrogant smile played across his face. "It seems to me that there is a certain ledge we found in a certain blizzard where you worked very hard to please me!"

Stepping back as if she were struck, Dana shouted at him as she strode toward the door. "I don't have to listen to this!"

"Wait! What about lunch?" he asked, oblivious to the hurt he had inflicted.

"Keep your lousy tuna sandwich." Her long legs took her rapidly out the front door and down the stairs.

In a flash he was at her side. "Wait a minute. Don't get mad. If you don't want tuna, I'll give you filet mignon." He grinned winningly, purposefully skirting the issue. "I know you're a good sport."

She stood statuelike on the bottom step. "A good sport is one thing. A doormat is another."

"No one could mistake you for a doormat."

Though she wanted to run away and knew she should, the sour taste in her mouth and the queasiness in her stomach wouldn't allow her to move. The climbing experience, even with all the pitfalls, and there had been many, was one of triumph, of ecstasy even. She didn't want it to end on this bitter note. She let him steer her, though she held herself woodenly rigid, back up the stairs and inside.

"Sit down," he ordered her. "I don't talk on an empty stomach. It's clear that we've got some talking to do."

With her hands folded primly in her lap and as neutral

170

an expression as she could muster, Dana sat quietly at his redwood breakfast table while he melted cheddar cheese on open-faced tuna.

"You'll share a split of champagne with me?" he asked as if the answer were a given.

She shook her head vehemently. "Give me apple juice. I'm not celebrating anything."

"We'll compromise." He took out a bottle of sparkling apple cider. "Now," he said as he poured the bubbly cider into fluted champagne glasses, "it seems we have a certain number of things to work out. I move that we approach them in a lawyerly fashion. So," he paused weightily, "why not begin by letting me see your briefs?"

Despite herself, Dana laughed. Between giggles she retorted, "Objection. The use of humor to disarm my righteous and well-deserved anger is unfair and unethical." She sobered as she recalled his earlier remarks at the hospital and here. She wasn't going to let him evade the issue with one-liners.

"First of all but not necessarily most important is the fact that I make my own decisions about what I do with my money and *nobody* influences me. For years I've been giving money away to causes that interest me. I started when I was six years old and adopted a bear at the Bronx Zoo. Instead of buying marbles and bubble gum like all my friends, I used to send my allowance to the zoo. And today the environment. Ecology is one of my primary interests. It's not that unrelated, you should be able to understand, to my passion for mountaineering. After all, I generally don't spend my vacations in cities breathing deeply of bus fumes. Granted, it's easier to sign and send off a check than to coordinate a campaign to preserve the land, but, Gary LeBlanc, though I may not be as worthy a person as you"—the voiced dripped sarcasm—"I'm not all that bad and selfish either!"

"Oh," he said. His head seemed to shrink down into his collar, reminding her of a turtle. She almost felt sorry for him.

"Furthermore . . ." She paused. "Eat your sandwich before it gets cold!"

Taking a big bite out of his sandwich, Gary looked thoughtful.

"Furthermore," she repeated, "my trust fund has always been a burden to me. I shouldn't feel that way, I suppose. True, I didn't do anything to earn the money, but my father did and he chose to give it to me. But somehow people like you, and, I guess, people like me, make me feel uneasy with it." She exhaled loudly.

"I didn't mean to make you uneasy, not about that anyway." He grinned. "I can see that I misjudged you about a couple of things, but you must admit, you make it easy to get the wrong idea."

"Why is that?"

"Your cheekbones, for example," he explained.

"What do my cheekbones have to do with anything?" she expostulated.

"Everything, my dear. Everything."

"That's an outrageous and ridiculous comment. I can see it's impossible to get through to you. It's no use talking anymore," Dana spat out, her face reddening.

"Don't get on your high horse again," Gary scowled. "What I meant is that your physical beauty is sometimes disconcerting. Besides, I didn't fill my apartment with Lladro and then much later admit that I hated the stuff. And I didn't prance around looking like a fashion plate while I examined climbing gear!" Gary finished his sandwich and made himself another. Noting that Dana had taken only one bite of hers, he continued, "What's the matter. You don't like my cooking?"

"There are other things about you that I like even less than your cooking and," she added pointedly, "I don't think I'm going to finish this sandwich."

"What do you like less than my cooking?" he asked mockingly, though his eyes betrayed a touch of vulnerability, a vulnerability that so contrasted with the hard strength of his usual demeanor that it weakened her resolve to continue the verbal sparring.

"Nothing," she mumbled. "Let's part friends. Your sandwich is fine. It's my appetite that's the problem." What was the use, anyway, she thought, dejected. The disparity in their feelings was enormous. That was plain to see. She was in love with this man, this great man of the mountains, and he liked her. Clearly he liked her. He was even physically attracted to her. But in love? No, he wasn't in love with her. He didn't even really respect her. Despite all of her protestations to the contrary, he thought of her as a Barbie doll who climbed mountains. In no way had he ever made her feel that he was madly, uncontrollably, in love with her. Oh, sure, she knew she was special to him in a way. It was clear when he had fished her from that glacial crevasse and pulled her out of the storm that he was badly shaken. But he wouldn't exactly have been whistling Dixie if it had been Joe or Bill who had almost been killed. So he had kissed her! Men kiss women all the time. And there was that undeniable physical magnetism that drew them to each other. But there was one startling incongruity in this whole mess, she thought morosely. Dana, the outsider, the despair of parents who wanted a cover-girl daughter to show off, had finally found and fallen prey to a man who was even more of an outsider than she. And he thought she represented everything he was rejecting. Well, someone had once said life was full of ironies. But, she argued with herself, he couldn't have been faking when he had made love to her. That was real and honest and intimate. She had never been so open to anyone before, and no one had ever given so much to her physically.

Well, Dana Manchester, she thought, you're more naive than you thought. Because a man made love to you, made glorious, tender love to you, you thought he loved you. Mother told you when you were pre-pubescent that there was a difference. Boys will be boys, she had said. And men will be men, Dana thought grimly. This was crazy. Why, after all, was she so hopelessly smitten with Gary? He had given her precious little fuel to fan the fires of this passion of hers. What she was suffering from was probably the student-professor syndrome. Every coed had at least one college crush on some uncombed, bespectacled professor who by virtue of the podium he stood behind was imbued with an unparalleled sexuality. As leader of the McKinley expedition, and the focus of her eyes for hours on end day after day, Gary's position was even more haloed than that of the most celebrated professor. She was forced to look at him until she was more familiar with his form, with his muscles, with his movements, than she was with her own. Her feelings for him were mere infatuation, she told herself, nothing more.

And then, as quickly as she had begun what she suddenly realized was a silly denial, she stopped it. She had never been good at lying to herself. After years of being alone, without a man to love, she had found Gary. And he was everything she had ever wanted in a man. He was capable, he was a leader among men, and he made his own way in life. There was only one problem. He didn't return her feelings. And he didn't think well enough of her. Unrequited love was a loser's game.

"Are you still here?" Gary broke into her reverie. "Ten thousand fifty dollars for your thoughts!" he said lightly.

"You wouldn't be interested, I don't think."

"You'd be surprised at how interested I am."

She hesitated. "I'm tired of thinking about myself. Tell me about you. If we never meet again," she laughed self-consciously, "I'd like to know more. Let's say for the record. For example, I don't quite understand why you dropped out of law school. You could have been a poor, dedicated lawyer or a famous prosecutor. It seems as if it were the action of a young rebel—not quite the way I see you."

"If we never meet again," he repeated her words with an odd smile. "So"—he changed his tone—"you want to know why I'm a law school dropout. Basically I told you already. I didn't enjoy the law and I didn't feel that I would make any real contribution as a lawyer. The Japanese who are astonished at the number of lawyers we Americans have are fond of saying that lawyers don't make the pie grow larger. They only decide how to cut it up. I don't suppose that owning a sporting goods store and guide service is adding to the pie in the same way as medical or mathematical research, but in my own way I like to think I'm contributing to the lives of the people I lead up those hills."

"I should say so!" Dana agreed vehemently. "So many who come climbing on their vacations lead the kind of lives where one day melts into the next and the end of what they're working for doesn't seem much different from the beginning. People like you and me give them the opportunity to realize a goal in a short time, to reach a summit. Those summits in other walks of life could take twenty years to attain."

"Right," Gary nodded. "But it's not only reaching that summit, Dana. The important thing is not necessarily to have won over that mountain, but to have fought well—to have, for a time, stripped life down to its essentials—to be able, in the final analysis, to keep putting one foot down in front of the other." His voice had a dreamy quality to it. "Did you want to climb when you were a kid?"

Dana shook her head.

"No? I did. I always wanted to climb, as long as I can remember. When I was in grade school I wanted to be the first person on top of the world's highest mountain. For about five years I daydreamed about that. Then someone told me Sir Edmund Hillary had already done it. So I decided that being first didn't matter. It was doing what I wanted that mattered. Other than getting sidetracked in law school for a couple of years, giving into family pressures, I've been fairly true to myself. My business gives me the time I want, and I don't have to answer to anyone. I was never much good at taking orders."

"You're good at giving them though," Dana said, smiling.

"Yes, I suppose I am."

The way he looked at her made her feel his mastery and his power. The blood pounded in her ears and her mouth felt dry. The strong legs that carried her to the highest peaks felt as if they would buckle. That he could seduce her with a look shook her to the core. And he knew it too. Therein lay the problem, or one of them. Feisty though she sounded, she was too malleable. He had made that clear when he had told her, albeit kiddingly, that she had worked hard to please him. The thought made her cringe. She wondered if he thought she was like that with other men. Perhaps she should tell him how long it had been since she had been with anyone and how she had always held back. But maybe it was all the same to him. But even if it did matter, she wouldn't want to appear as if she were pleading her case. To beg for his love was something she would never do anyway. She would rather end up alone with twenty cats to warm her bed.

He cleared his throat. "Confessions aren't my style. There is something you ought to know about the LeBlanc family though. True, we have a knack for making money. We also have a knack for being cold. It's easier to go against a family's wishes," he said ruefully, "than to learn a new life script." He cracked his knuckles, a gesture she had never seen him do before. "What I'm trying to say is that if I appear unfeeling . . ."

"It's because you are!" she finished.

Exasperation was etched in his face. "Never mess with a woman from Scarsdale! That's a lesson I've learned."

It was as if something snapped inside her head. Moving jerkily from the kitchen area toward the fireplace, she whirled to him. "How come you say that you're unlearning the lessons of your background but you don't believe the same of me? You've never taken me seriously."

"That's not true," he objected. "I wouldn't have included you in the expedition had I not taken you seriously."

Dana felt like laughing and crying at the same time. Damn him! She wasn't talking about climbing now! Exasperation bordering on despair claimed her.

"Good," she said tartly. "I'm glad we've got that straightened out. I had better get going now, Gary.

There's a lot of things I have to do before I leave. Thanks for lunch."

As she headed toward the door she felt his viselike grip on her arm.

"Are we going to play the same scene over and over—you trying to leave and me stopping you?" His face was menacingly close. She stared up at him in amazement. Twisting a handful of her hair in his hand, his mouth swooped down to take possession of hers. With his tongue he parted her lips. It was so easy to yield to him. So easy. With all the will she could garner she pulled back.

"No, don't!"

"Why not?" he asked lazily.

"I don't want you to make love to me, not like this."

"I'll do it any way you want," he teased, his hand caressing her neck in gentle circles. "I can think of dozens of ways to make love to you." His voice was creamy soft, more intimate than a caress.

Lifting his hand from her neck, she averted her eyes. A lump rose in her throat. "Don't you understand?" she whispered chokingly.

He raked his hand through his own hair. "I think I do," he answered. "Dana, oh, Dana. You're a wonderful woman. A bit insecure, but a wonderful woman. And yes, to finally answer your question. I know you're not the woman I thought at first. I'm quite certain you couldn't care less if you never tasted crepes suzette again in your life. I'm also certain you know what you're running away from. I'm not sure you know what you're running to though. You won't want to spend all your winters doing office temp work. My business is expanding, especially the mountaineering guide service," he said almost as if he were talking to himself. "I could use a partner."

Shaking her head as if she were hearing things, Dana wrinkled her nose. He couldn't be proposing a business partnership to her! So that he wouldn't know how close she was to emotional collapse, she answered brashly, "You're not only one of the country's foremost mountaineers, you're also a career counselor! My, you certainly are a man for all seasons! Oh, and how much money did you want me to put up for my half of the business?"

As soon as the words were out, Dana could have bitten her tongue. She knew he wasn't trying to get at her money. It was as if, hurt and down, she were striking out blindly, not caring where her blows landed.

Recoiling from her as from a venomous serpent, Gary turned away. But not before the curtain fell over his eyes.

"I'm sorry, Gary. I didn't mean to say that. I don't know why I did. I . . ."

"If I don't see one red cent of your money it will be too much. Do you understand?" His voice was brittle.

Burying her face in her hands, Dana thought miserably that his anger was justified. She had wrecked whatever small hope had been left to work things out—to give love a try. But, she thought again, as a climber, hadn't she always kept up the struggle knowing full well that the balance between success and failure was delicate? Why, in love, should she be less a woman than she was on the mightiest mountains?

"Let me explain," she said in a small voice.

"Not necessary," he replied tightly.

"I love you," she said.

In slow motion, it seemed, he turned to face her. What she saw in his eyes was unmistakable. They sparkled with a splendid joy as they had when he stood so proudly on

McKinley's summit. He seemed, if anything, more animated now.

"Would you repeat that, please?" he asked, incredulous.

"I love you."

And then his lips were on hers, clinging, burning, sealing her words with his kiss. Her world seemed to explode with rapturous delight. He didn't have to say anything. A kiss like his, warm, tender, worshipping, demanding, did not lie.

"We can work it out," she whispered breathlessly between kisses.

"There's nothing to work out," he slurred as he nibbled at the corner of her bottom lip. "Everything's perfect."

She pulled back slightly. "We do have things to discuss," she said with a warm smile.

"Mmm-hmm. We'll put Lladro in every room of the house," Gary muttered.

"I told you twice already that I hate Lladro," she laughed jubilantly, "and what house?"

"Our house. The one we'll design and have built when you tell me that you'll marry me."

"Marry you?" she repeated as though the words had not penetrated.

"I love you too," he said. "Strangely enough, that first time I saw you sitting there in the Oak Room at the Plaza, I knew I was a goner."

"Is that why you were so mean to me?" she asked coquettishly. "You were fighting the inevitable?" She knew she was prattling and didn't care. All that she could think of was that he loved her! He loved her!

He laughed gruffly. "Remember what I told you about the LeBlanc family? Now, don't get used to honeyed words and endearments."

"Well then, you had better not get used to a warm bed!" she teased. "We both have to learn to compromise!"

"Uh-uh." He shook his head though his eyes twinkled. "I lead and you follow."

"Only on Mount McKinley!"

"How about Rainier, the Tetons, and Everest?"

"I'll grant you the mountains," she laughed. "But I have the lowlands."

"Did I tell you our house is going to be on top of a mountain?" he chuckled.

At her slightly worried frown, his chuckle grew into a laugh. "Don't worry. We're a team." Gathering her in his arms he hugged her. "Will you be able to stand living in Alaska?" he asked as though the thought of her discontent alarmed him.

"I'd be able to stand the North Pole with you," she smiled. "Anyway, I love Fairbanks."

"We'll make lots of trips into New York," he answered as though he didn't believe her. "I go on business three or four times a year anyway. You'll be able to see your parents and—"

"Don't say it," she cut him off laughingly, "My Lladro?"

He kissed her again. "Did I ever tell you how much I like you? Besides loving you? You're smart and funny and brave and strong." He gave her a crooked grin. "You're also pretty good in the . . . sleeping bag!"

"Gary!" she reproved him indignantly.

"Speaking of which . . ." He pulled her gently toward him.

"Gary, Gary . . ." Dana seemed to protest.

"Don't worry, Bill and Joe can't hear," Gary said smilingly. "Come this way. Beautiful as the sleeping bag was, there's nothing wrong with a bed either." Gary's strong arms encircled Dana's waist as he scooped her up and carried her into the bedroom. As he lowered her into his bed, she held on to his neck and pulled him on top of her.

"By the way, I like you a lot too. Besides loving you. And"—Dana hesitated for effect—"you're so good in the kitchen. That was a mean tuna 'n' cheese you whipped up."

Gary's lips were upon hers with a long, hungry kiss. "You, my dear, beautiful lady, are going to take your clothes off," Gary said in a light way, yet with a commanding undertone.

"Aye, aye, sir. On the double," Dana continued.

As Gary himself undressed he devoured her with his eyes, from her long, slim legs to her stunningly beautiful face and intense yet laughing eyes. "Lie down here," he said so simply and strongly that Dana was helpless to resist. For a full minute Gary merely looked at her, a look that gave her almost more anticipatory pleasure than Dana could stand. It seemed to Dana that Gary saw her completely to her core. Finally he lay alongside her and they lightly kissed, their bodies barely touching. Tracing the fine lines of her neck and collarbone with his thumb, Gary kissed her lips. Dana shuddered at the feel of his body against her. She gasped as his mouth lowered to her breasts, closing first upon one hard nipple then the other. His tongue teasingly flicked over the sensitive flesh, leaving her with a drawing sensation of exquisite pleasure. Their strong supple bodies luxuriated in each other as Dana answered Gary's kisses hungrily. Her passion ignited by Gary's proposal and the realization that her dreams were coming true, Dana moaned softly, "Gary, I want you. Make love to me. Make love to me now."

"And I want you too." Gary punctuated his assertion with a slow, sweet invasion. Savoring the exquisite sensations, they moved hardly at all, then gradually and with their own rhythm they began what Dana fleetingly thought of as a love ballet. Gary's hands raised hers over her head as their bodies conformed to each other.

As they rocked rhythmically, Dana felt overwhelmed by the elemental sensations that coursed through her body and by the primitive emotions she felt so viscerally. This man was hers. She was his. Running her fingers through Gary's hair and over his back, twisting his curls around her fingers and kneading his muscles, Dana moaned inarticulately but expressively. She knew she belonged to him as she could never belong to any other man. Opening herself totally and unconditionally to him, Dana lost all consciousness of herself. His chest, her legs and breasts, his arms—everything was an undifferentiated body of love, she thought rapturously.

As he thrust deeply into her, his hands never ceased to touch and stroke her shoulders, her throat, the soft flesh of her inner thighs, her buttocks. Once, as he slowed and shortened his frenzied movements, she caught him looking over his shoulder at her legs. He shook his head in wonderment and reverentially he stroked the shapely limbs that were extended straight up in the air.

"You have the best legs in the western world, woman," he said softly.

"I have the best man," she answered.

Separating from her, he lowered his face to her thighs. She thought she would faint from pleasure as his lips and tongue worshipped her.

"You're so good to me," he moaned, "so sweet." Handling her gently, yet with a proprietary sense, he turned her over on her stomach. "Do you know what I'm going to do now?" he murmured.

"Yes," she whispered.

"No, I don't think you do. I want to see you, all of you." He proceeded to explore her with his hands and with his eyes. For interminable minutes he held her, he touched her, he felt her quiver under his touch.

Dana closed her eyes. Never had she been so exposed, so vulnerable. She thought that she ought to hold back, but all she felt was the desire to make him happy and to fulfill her own happiness.

And then with a groan, the sound itself sending a thrill of satisfaction coursing through her, Gary turned her on her back again. Clasping her wrists, he joined with her, this time with deep, quickening, unstoppable thrusts that shattered her last ounce of self-control. She could feel the explosion building inside her and felt her hands pushing against his as it came, sending them together into a maelstrom of utter bliss.

"You're a strong woman. I like that."

She smiled.

"That, you know, was the real taste of heaven."

"I love you, Gary," Dana said with simple contentment.

"And I love you, Mrs. LeBlanc."

CHAPTER ELEVEN

As Gary and Dana stood before her mother in the foyer of the Scarsdale mansion, Dana thought of last night. Gary had insisted that they spend it at the Plaza. The next day, he had insisted, was soon enough to meet her parents. After drinks at the Oak Bar, the site of their first meeting, she had teased him relentlessly about what she termed his hopeless romanticism. Back in their suite he had, with the same relentlessness, made love to her. As a result, Dana had been bleary-eyed all morning.

"Mother, I'd like you to meet Gary LeBlanc," Dana announced proudly, one hand resting on Gary's arm, the other on her mother's.

"Pleased to meet you, Mrs. Manchester. I've heard so much about you." Gary was wearing his polite, social personality.

"I hear from Dana that you climb mountains. How exciting! Dana's always been interested in climbing too," her mother exclaimed not quite convincingly. She was dimly aware of Dana's intentions.

"Mother, Gary and I are going to get married."

"Oh, isn't that wonderful." After a little awkward hesitation, Mrs. Manchester continued. "So Mr. LeBlanc, what is your profession?"

"I climb mountains," Gary said simply, "and please call me Gary."

"But Gary," Mrs. Manchester tried to disguise her feelings, "I don't understand. Is there much money in climbing mountains?" She laughed nervously.

"Money, no. Reward, yes. I do have a sporting goods store in Fairbanks which I mind when I'm not climbing. That will buy us food and put a roof over our heads," Gary answered with his usual modesty.

Dana laughed. "It's a huge store, Mother, and with it, climbing, and his environmental interests, Gary's got his hands full."

"You forgot my main interest, Dana," Gary winked. "You."

Dana smiled but was disturbed by her mother's attitude.

"Mr. Manchester will gladly put you through law or medical school or even business school if you prefer. It's never too late."

Gary cast Dana a bemused smile, but Dana was clearly annoyed.

"Mother!" she said sharply.

"Mrs. Manchester," Gary interjected, "could you show me some of your Lladro. Dana's told me so much about it."

"Why, yes, come over here." Mrs. Manchester looked

186

pleased for the first time. "Look at this Don Quixote. Isn't it exquisite. The lines are so fine and flowing."

Gary was glad to be off the subject of his proposed retraining for polite society, and was happy to see genuine enthusiasm in any form. "I like that grayish-rose-colored porcelain. Very nice."

Mollified by his interest in the figurines, Mrs. Manchester ordered that some snacks be brought in. "Maybe you'd be interested in managing a weight-loss center that Mr. Manchester has just bought?" she chirped. "There's a nice little Tudor for sale not half a mile from here."

Unable to contain herself any longer, Dana burst out, "Mother, I love you and Daddy very much, but you must understand that I'm not you and Gary is not Daddy. You have your life and I have mine," she paused, "or, rather, we have ours, and ours we've decided will be in Alaska—climbing, running Gary's store and guide service, and protecting the environment so far as we can. And I have to say that I'm not going to pretend anymore about things. We have very different ideas of beauty. Neither is better than the other—only different. So, please, Mother when you send gifts, and I do appreciate your thinking of me, don't send anything breakable. A box of Godiva chocolates on my birthday would be a real treat. I doubt if they sell that in Alaska. And most important, Mother, don't try to change me anymore and don't ever try to change anything about Gary, not even one hair on his head."

Her mother stood open-mouthed as if rooted to the floor. "Why, I never dreamed!"

"Don't worry, Mrs. Manchester, I'll make your daughter happy. I won't be taking her away for good. We'll get back a few times a year on sporting goods business. I have most of my contacts here in New York. And when you come out to visit us in Fairbanks, we'll be glad to guide you and Mr. Manchester up some gentle slopes. Maybe you'll even get a taste of the appeal of the mountains."

Dana looked at Gary and their eyes locked.

A split of champagne and a box of Godiva chocolates were waiting for them in their Plaza suite, courtesy of the elder Manchesters.

"At heart she's a dear," Dana said fondly.

"She wants the best for you. She's just a little off course," Gary agreed. "So you want gifts of chocolate from your parents. What kind of gifts do you want from me?"

"You," she answered as she slid her arms around his neck.

"You've got that already," he answered. "You know what I'm going to give you for your birthday every year?"

"What?" she asked smilingly.

"A climb. And since we've already done the highest North American peak together, for the next six years we'll do the highest summit on each of the remaining six continents."

"What a magnificent plan!" She kissed him. "But what happens if I get pregnant?" With her arms still draped around his neck she stood away.

"I'll be the happiest man on the planet. And we'll postpone our climbs."

"Oh? For how long, nine months, a year?" she asked.

When he answered it was with a lopsided grin that she found irresistible. "Until the kid finishes law school!"

Exploding with laughter, they rolled on the bed, kissing and tickling and loving.

Candlelight

Ecstasy Romances™

$1.95 each

At your local bookstore or use this handy coupon for ordering:

DELL BOOKS
P.O. BOX 1000, PINE BROOK, N.J. 07058-1000   B184A

Please send me the books I have checked above I am enclosing $_____ (please add 75c per copy to cover postage and handling) Send check or money order—no cash or C.O.D.'s Please allow up to 8 weeks for shipment

Name _____

Address _____

City _____ State Zip _____

CANDLELIGHT Ecstasy Supreme

$2.50 each

CANDLELIGHT Ecstasy Supreme

$2.50 each